Catherine E Hurst

Queen Louisa of Prussia

Catherine E Hurst

Queen Louisa of Prussia

ISBN/EAN: 9783337171094

Printed in Europe, USA, Canada, Australia, Japan

Cover: Foto ©Raphael Reischuk / pixelio.de

More available books at **www.hansebooks.com**

CONTENTS.

QUEEN LOUISA OF PRUSSIA.

I.

The Goethe Family—Frankfort-on-the-Main.

OWARD the close of the last century two princely children might have been seen in the Grosse Hirschgrabenstrasse, Frankfort-on-the-Main, where they were amusing themselves by pumping water from an old mediæval pump in the door-yard. When the chief servant saw them she was greatly enraged, as might very well be supposed, and immediately called them away; but the good old lady who was entertaining the children bade her servant let them alone. The servant, however, was not willing to obey, whereupon the good hostess locked her up in a room, and let the children pump as much as they wished. This was certainly a great triumph for the little folks, and when they came to take their departure, they thanked their much-loved friend for her great kindness, and said they would never forget their delightful visit.

Later in life this indulgent and kind woman was rewarded by one of her guests with a costly gold ornament, which the recipient considered too valuable to be worn except on festal occasions. The jewel was kept as a great family treasure.

One of these children, Louisa, the subject of this sketch, became the wife of William III., King of Prussia; and the kind lady who entertained her was Frau Rath Goethe, mother of the great German poet, John Wolfgang Goethe.

We are not surprised at the leniency of Frau Goethe, when we consider that, nearly twoscore years before, she had enjoyed with great delight the innocent sports of her own children, and never wearied in uniting with them in their childish amusements. She was always as playful as any of the number. We mention one out of many amusing incidents illustrating her indulgent and child-like disposition.

One day, when John Wolfgang, her eldest child, was about three years of age, and his parents were worshiping at church, Master Wolfgang found himself in the kitchen, which opened out upon the street. In making a selection in that forbidden spot of what would give him the most pleasure, boy-like, he concluded to throw the kitchen crockery out on the pavement, and enjoy the "smashing music" which it would make. When he saw the neighbors, the brothers Von Ochsenstein, the surviving sons of the deceased imperial councilor, on the opposite side of the street, laughing at him, he felt greatly encouraged, and continued making the plates and dishes fly in all directions, until his mother returned from church. Frau Goethe, on entering the house, immediately saw the mischief with a housewifely horror ; but melting into girlish sympathy as she saw how heartily little Wolfgang laughed at his escapade, and how the neighbors enjoyed the sport, she entered into the scene with as much enthusiasm as the boy himself.*

While this may seem a great destruction of property, it must be remembered that German kitchens are supplied cheaply from the *Messe*, or fair, which occurs twice during the year. During these fairs, which continue three weeks in spring and autumn, the street in Frankfort bordering on the river Main is lined on either side with the earthen and stone crockery, and here the good German housewives can replenish or furnish in full their entire kitchen for a few dollars.

Nine years after Louisa's first visit to Frau Rath Goethe at Frankfort-on-the Main, we find

* Lewes, Life and Works of Goethe, pp. 18, 19.

her with the king on their return from a tour through Westphalia, spending a few days in this imperial city with Louisa's sister, the Princess Theresa, who was visiting her husband's relatives. This sister had married Prince Alexander of Thurn and Taxis, and his parents resided at Frankfort-on-the-Main, in their beautiful palace, standing near the grand old Eschenheimer Tower, which still bears their name.[*]

Frau Rath Goethe describes this visit to a friend in a letter written July 28, 1799:

"Their majesties have been with us at Frankfort, and we have done what we could to welcome them. I had a very unexpected honor. The queen sent her brother to me with a kind invitation to come and see her. The prince came in the afternoon, and sat down and dined with me at my small table.

"At six o'clock we went in his carriage, with

* HUDSON, Louisa, Queen of Prussia, vol. i, p. 221.

two footmen behind us, to the palace of Thurn and Taxis. The queen received me with great kindness, and talked of the old times and the pleasure I had given her in my old house in the Grosse Hirschgrabenstrasse."

Frankfort had suffered much during the war, having been captured by the French. The inhabitants had been cruelly burdened, and some of them quite impoverished, by oppressive taxes, and the heavy expense of having troops quartered upon them. Frau Rath Goethe had suffered so much that she found herself obliged to sell her large house on the Grosse Hirschgrabenstrasse, and occupy a smaller one on the Ross Market. She was living in this small house when the king and queen visited the Princess Alexander.

Although Frau Goethe was no longer able to exercise that unbounded liberality and hospitality congenial to her disposition, she bore her vexations with great equanimity, always looking on the bright side of life and human nature.

She clung to every pleasant thing around her, and much of her time was agreeably spent in corresponding with her son and her large circle of friends, which included persons of the highest rank in both the social and literary world. Those of her letters which have been preserved are so like her, that through them we may know her intimately, and "to know her is to love her."

Frau Rath Goethe was a widow, and John Wolfgang, the poet, was now her only surviving child, and he was the joy and pride of her heart. He was in the prime of life, one of the great men of the day, the brightest ornament of the court of Saxe-Weimar, "the Athens of Germany," where his genius was fully appreciated. Her daughter Cornelia lived to become the wife of the historian, Schlosser, but died soon after her marriage.

Bettina von Arnim, in one of her letters to the poet Goethe, amusingly describes a visit that she made to his mother. Bettina was

2

greatly attached to, and on very intimate terms with, the old lady. She writes:

"When I called, your mother was not at home, but as the servant who opened the door said that she was expecting her mistress soon to return, I took the liberty of walking into the room to the right of the hall. It was very nearly dark, and after I had waited in silence for some time, I thought I heard sounds, as if some creature were moving or breathing in the room. I fancied it must be the squirrel which had been left by a French prisoner at your mother's house when he was quartered there. This little animal was a great pet with your mother, and he had become very audacious, and was up to all kinds of mischief. He had even dared to sit on her best head-dress, and to nibble the feathers and ribbon.

"Bettina, hearing mysterious sounds, called the squirrel by name, 'Hanschen, Hanschen, are you there?'

"'It is not Hanschen, but Hans,' answered

a deep voice from the further end of the room.

"'Then,' says Bettina, 'I felt quite abashed, for I knew it was no less a person than Queen Louisa's brother, the Prince of Mecklenburg, but the darkness covered my confusion, and a moment after your mother came in, exclaiming, 'Are you there?'

"'Yes!' we exclaimed both together, and in the twilight I then saw a youth with a star on his breast.

"'Frau Rath, may I eat a bacon-salad and pancakes with you this evening?' said the prince.

"She answered in the affirmative, in her usually pleasant way."

About this time Louisa's father, Prince Charles Frederic, presented Frau Goethe with a very handsome snuff-box as a token for her kindness to his children. The old lady, who maintained her position as a councilor's widow, had a box at the theater next to the king's box.

One evening as she was sitting there enjoying the play, and from time to time refreshing herself with a pinch of snuff, (then the custom,) and wishing the king, his sons, and other royal personages occupying their box to notice her snuff-box, she put it forward, and tapped it audibly, but for some time they did not observe it. She describes with much vivacity her various maneuvers to attract attention. At last the king said:

"What a beautiful snuff-box you have, Frau Rath Goethe!"

"Yes, your majesty," she replied, "and it was given to me in remembrance of my dear princesses of Mecklenburg."

Louisa and Frau Goethe one day engaged in a long discussion on German literature. The pleasure that the queen had from her girlhood derived from Goethe's works, especially from his simpler poems, deepened the interest that she felt in his mother. Yielding to the sentiment of the moment, Louisa unclasped an elegant gold necklace that she was wearing on her neck, and gave it to the poet's mother as a tribute to the power of genius, and at the same time as a souvenir of the many pleasant hours spent in her society.

Frau Rath, observing one evening that this brilliant ornament had attracted the attention of Madame de Stäel, said, with her characteristic naïveté, "Oui, je suis la mère de Goethe."

In the summer of 1870, as we were wending our way to the cemetery, in the suburbs of Frankfort, to visit the last resting-place of our beloved daughter Clara, a friend inquired if we had ever seen the old cemetery. On our answering in the negative, she immediately directed our steps thither. We had walked but a short distance, after passing through the quaint gate, when our attention was called to a very old, plain-looking grave. As we stooped down to read the inscription on the recumbent stone slab, which lay almost even with the ground, we were surprised to find the following :—

FRAU RATH GOETHE, (geb. Textor.)
Born February 19, 1731.
Died September 13, 1808.   .

We could scarcely realize that we were standing beside the grave of the mother of him who shares with Schiller the high honor of having written the best poetry of the Fatherland. For sixty-two years that admired and genial woman had been sleeping that sleep that "knows no waking." It would seem that her very love of children and sympathy with their sports were continued after death. As the old grave-yard lies between two important sections of the city, many of the school children pass twice every day back and forth through it, and often stop and take their lunch and play their games upon or near the well-worn tombstone.

There is no doubt that the beautiful relation of Louisa, when a child, to the Goethe family had a very important influence on her later life, and that it was one of the impulses which controlled her, many years afterward, when she had become a queen, in her cultivation of the acquaintance of literary people, and particularly in aiding and encouraging worthy young aspirants to excellence in letters. Her latest biographer, in describing this feature of her social life and character, says:

" Goethe makes one of these Mecklenburg princesses in his Tasso say, 'I am always happy to hear clever people conversing;' and these words describe Queen Louisa's taste, for although she conversed sensibly, fluently, and without constraint, yet she preferred listening to expressing her own ideas. . . .

" The palaces that she and the king occupied were open to statesmen, military men, distinguished professors, artists, and authors. . . . The queen's natural capacity and highly cultivated mind enabled her to take pleasure in such society, although she was entirely free from all affectation and pedantry. ^She had modest views of her own abilities and opinions, and sought to improve her own mind by bringing out the minds of others. Her conversation, as well as her whole behavior, was gently but beautifully guided with that feminine tact which never failed her, because it sprang from an ever-present desire to avoid giving the slightest pain or annoyance to others. She was always ready to converse with any one, always perfectly at ease, and her lively, genial manner was all the more winning because she was unconscious that she was attracting admiration." *

* HUDSON, Louisa, Queen of Prussia, vol. ii, pp. 22, 27, 29, 30, 95.

II.

Louisa's Youth.

N collecting the incidents of Queen Louisa's life we are not surprised to find that the German people were enthusiastically fond of her, and that poets vied with each other in singing her praises. She had grown up in German simplicity, and had stored her mind with the best literature that the nation had to offer. When these advantages, crowned by the warm influences of religion, appeared united in the person of a young, beautiful, affable, and loving queen, how could her people do otherwise than love and praise her?

It was her fortune to live in the darkest period of Prussia's history, and few n that kingdom suffered so much from its shame and ruin; yet she hoped without wavering, and strove to encourage in all the firm belief that, by God's assistance, the nation would, Phœnix-like, rise out of its ruins to a new and nobler life, purified by the fire of affliction it had endured, and strengthened by its sufferings.

If Prussia stands to-day at the head of European nations, a large portion of its advancement is traceable directly to the enthusiasm inspired by her earnest life, willing sacrifices, and fervent prayers. During the late war between Germany and France her memory was revived in the hearts of the people of the Fatherland in a remarkable manner. The periodicals abounded in biographies of her. Her portrait could be seen at the windows of the picture stores ; and so frequent were the references to her, that she seemed to be still among the living rather than the dead. She *was* living—for, though dead in appearance, she was still speaking.

But in order to show how she attained such a place of honor and love in the hearts of her

people—not only of her own, but of the suc-
ceeding generation—it will be necessary to trace
her history with some degree of minuteness.

On the 10th of March, 1776, Louisa Augusta
Wilhelmina Amelia, Princess of Mecklenburg,
was born in Hanover. She was descended
from one of the oldest and most famous
princely families of Germany, for to her ancestors belonged the great Henry the Lion, of
the house of Guelph, who lived in the twelfth
century. The latter gave his daughter in marriage to the uncle of the last Wendish and
Obotrite king, from whom came the Mecklenburg line of princes.

Louisa's father was Charles Louis Frederic,
Field Marshal, and Governor-General of Han-
over. He was also reigning duke from the
year 1794, and Grand Duke of Mecklenburg-
Strelitz from the year 1815. The mother was
Frederica Caroline Louisa, daughter of George,
Landgrave of Hesse-Darmstadt. Louisa was
the sixth child of these parents.

She, with her brothers and sisters, suffered a severe loss in early life. Their mother died on the 22d of May, 1782, when Louisa was but six years of age. The afflicted father went with his six children to the castle of Herrenhausen, which lies near Hanover. In this beautiful chateau, surrounded by the most exquisite gardens, he lived for some years in rural simplicity. He felt it his duty, however, later to marry again, that his children, who were still young, might have the benefit of a mother's love and care. He accordingly married the sister of his deceased wife, the Princess Charlotte Wilhelmina Christina, on the 21st of September, 1784, at Darmstadt. Louisa was present at the marriage, and remained at Darmstadt during the following winter with her relatives. Her healthy, joyous nature won the hearts of all. In the summer she returned to her parents in their palace at Herrenhausen.

The duke and his children were very soon again called to pass through severe affliction.

On the 12th of December, 1785, the duchess died, having been permitted but fourteen months to have charge of her sister's children. She left an infant, Charles of Mecklenburg, who afterward became Prussian General of Infantry, and chief of the Guards. He distinguished himself in the War of Liberation against Napoleon I., particularly at Katzbach and Leipsig, and died in Berlin in the year 1839.

After the death of the duchess the duke bade farewell to Hanover, and took his children to Darmstadt, where they could have the loving care of their grandmother. She was a true woman in heart and soul, and did every thing in her power to develop the intellectual abilities of these motherless children, and lead them in the ways of virtue and religion. She selected, as governess for Louisa, Fräulein Gelieur, a Swiss lady of superior worth. This individual accomplished her task satisfactorily, and Louisa showed her gratitude to her governess by a life-long attachment.

Only once in after times did the queen complain of her education — that it was more French than German. It was the custom in those times among the aristocracy to use the French language, and follow the French fashions. The German language and German usages were not considered genteel enough. Louisa deeply regretted that she had in her childhood imbibed this false idea, and she exerted herself later in life to retrieve the error. Apart from this, her education was well directed.

She was easily brought to a child-like adoration of God and admiration of his great works, and was taught the truly royal way of well-doing. With her governess accompanying her, Louisa was allowed to visit the cottages of the poor and the bedsides of the suffering. Often did she bring joy to the hearts of the sick and needy by her gifts, and dry the tears of the sorrowful by her gentleness and loving smiles. Thus early did she practice that humanity and

Visiting the Sick.

courtesy which, in later years, won for her all hearts.

The attachment of Louisa to this governess, Fräulein Gelieur, was intense, and suffered no abatement after the pupil became a queen. The governess, however, survived Louisa, and after her death her husband, the king, carried out a cherished wish to express personally his gratitude for the life-long interest which the Fräulein had manifested in the one who had been to him a loving and devoted wife. After the allied monarchs had made their entrance into Paris, in 1815, as victors over Napoleon, Frederic William, with the crown prince, made his homeward journey through Switzerland, in part to see the princedom of Neuchatel, but more particularly to visit the aged governess of the late queen. Fräulein Gelieur lived in an obscure village called Colombier, on the lake of Neuchatel, with her brother, who was pastor of the place. What a joyful surprise when she recognized in that unostentatious officer the husband of her former pupil! After the horrors of war and the festivities of victory, the king wished to give an hour to the melancholy yet loving remembrance of his never-to-be-forgotten Louisa. On his departure he gave to the old lady, besides several other handsome presents, an expensive shawl, which the queen had worn only a short time before her death. This beautiful gift moved the governess to tears.

We find an exquisite and affecting story, which is taken from the "Mühlheimer Chronicle," illustrating Louisa's character when a child. The incident occurred while she lived at Mühlheim with her grandmother, the landgravine from Hesse. The children of the servants belonging to the royal household were allowed to play in the palace garden with the Princesses Louisa and Frederica, and their governess often went with them to visit these children living in the neighborhood of the palace. Louisa was never happier than when allowed to partake with her playmates of their homely meal of black bread and thick milk, and join with them in their innocent sports.

One day, as they were playing in the palace garden, a thunder-storm came on very unexpectedly. The lightning and thunder were terrific, and each mother from the different tenement houses hurried to the palace garden to take her children home. One little girl, named Hannah, was left behind, for she had no mother. She was the daughter of the first läufer (a running footman, who must keep pace with a carriage) of the landgravine, and who was cared for by an aunt, who had no affection for her. When the Princess Louisa saw that she had no protector she took Hannah in her arms to a place of shelter, and said to her,

"Be quiet, dear Hannah; do not be afraid of the thunder and lightning and rain, for our dear Saviour sends it; and do not be sad, for you are not alone. I am with you,

3

and your father will come soon and take you home."

Hannah, looking earnestly in Louisa's face, replied,

"Who will take care of me when my father dies?"

"Who says that your father will die?" quickly answered the little princess.

"Oh, my aunt says that he suffers so much from pain in his breast when he must run so rapidly to keep pace with the horses, and that he can live but a very short time."

Louisa was shocked at this reply, and turned quite pale. She had never for one moment thought, when driving out in her grandmother's elegant equipages, that the brilliantly-dressed läufer, with his golden saber at his side, running so gracefully, could ever become fatigued. Now for the first time in her life she considered the subject, and pressing little Hannah near her heart, large tears found their way down her rosy cheeks, falling on her little friend's forehead. She embraced Hannah more tenderly, and told her to be very quiet, for she did not wish to see her weeping.

"Be assured," she continued, "your father shall not die; for I will tell this to grandma, and she will give him another position."

When evening came, and Louisa was in the presence of her grandmother, she quickly related, with tears streaming from her eyes, Hannah's simple story about her father, and told her grandmother that she could never more have any pleasure in driving while she knew that the footmen were sacrificing their health in consequence of it. She continued further, weeping bitterly:

"O, grandma, I know that you can have no more pleasure, either, now that you know how much these poor men suffer. Will you not think about it?"

The grandmother patted her sweet grandchild's cheek, and, with soothing and encouraging words, sent the child to bed.

The good landgravine then paced her room in deep thought, and never again was she seen with footmen attending her carriage during her pleasure drives. This barbarous custom of the mediæval times was, in that royal household, from that time abandoned.

A short time after the above occurrence the scarlet fever, in its most malignant form, appeared in Mühlheim and the surrounding country. The groups of children who were accustomed to play in the palace garden became smaller and smaller. One after another of them was attacked with the fearful disease, and many of them were laid in their little graves. One day Hannah was missed from the circle, and the news soon came that she, too, had become a victim to this dreaded disease. The landgravine gave orders that a physician should attend her daily, and report to the palace. Days, and even weeks, passed without any hope of the recovery of the little sick one. Finally, one day, greatly to the joy

of all in the palace, the physician reported that
the fever had left her, and she would very soon
recover. A few days later the landgravine felt
that it would be safe to visit the little friend of
her granddaughter. As she came near the
läufer's house she saw that the window of the
sick room was raised, and the curtain drawn
aside. She looked in unobserved, and, to her
great surprise, found her grandchild Louisa sitting at the foot of the bed reading to her little
playmate, while Hannah was amusing herself
with the princess' embroidered pocket-handker-
chief. The landgravine did not enter, but left
unobserved, as she had came. We can well
imagine her very great anxiety at beholding
her granddaughter in this sick room, exposed
to the frightful disease.

Louisa had great taste for sketching from
nature, and was allowed an hour each day to
go out alone while the governess was otherwise
engaged with her sister. She had taken advantage of this hour, and had been in the habit

during Hannah's illness of visiting her whenever it was possible to find admittance to the
sick room.

When Louisa returned home the grandmother said,

"Where have you been, my child?"

Looking up at her very much frightened, she
replied,

"O, grandma, I have been with a sick child,
who has no mother and no grandmother like
you are, and who would have died long ago if
I had not visited her. Will you not forgive
me, dear grandma, for not telling you of my
visits to her before?"

"You know, my child, this disease could so
easily have taken you from us, and what would
we then do? Oh, the grief we would have at
your loss!" said the old lady, giving way to con-
vulsive sobbing, and embracing her loved one.

"I knew well," replied Louisa, "that I would
not get the disease, for der liebe Gott—the dear
God—saw that I was doing good."

Now we must return to Louisa's later youth.
It was a great joy to her that in her fourteenth year she was allowed to make a visit to
her aunt, wife of the Count Palatine, Maximilian
of Zweibrucken, who was living at Strasburg.
Louisa possessed an unusually deep apprecia-
tion of the charms of nature, as well as of
every thing that was beautiful. She was particularly attracted by the magnificence of the
great minster at Strasburg, and wished to
ascend the three hundred and twenty-five steps
which lead to the platform roof of the cathedral,
that she might enjoy the extended view presented there. Her grandmother, after a little
hesitation, gave her consent, and on reaching
the place, Louisa was so delighted that she
wished to mount the other four hundred steps,
which lead to the very top of the tower. But
when the governess told her she felt giddy, and
dare not go further, Louisa immediately yielded, and returned with her.

Louisa's two visits to Frankfort-on-the-Main

were among her most pleasant recollections. They took place during the coronation of the two last German emperors, Leopold II., on the 1st of September, 1790, and Francis I., on the 17th of July, 1792.

These coronations were magnificent festive occasions. The State jewelry was brought from Nuremburg and Aix-la-Chapelle to the cathedral in a coach drawn by six span of horses. The new emperor rode from his palace to the same place in magnificent procession, preceded by the electors in their official robes, surrounded by the deputies of the city, bearing a canopy over him, the officers of the court by his side, and his body-guards and the city guards following. Bringing up the rear— on foot, on horseback, and in carriages—came the emperor's and the electors' followers, while banners were flying and drums constantly sounding. Having arrived at the cathedral, the king stood on the high altar and took the oath on the Four Gospels, (the copy belonging to Aix-la-Chapelle,) while high mass was being performed. Then he was anointed by the Elector of Mayence, in archiepiscopal robes, having the sword of Charles V. girt about him. After partaking of the Lord's Supper, he ascended to the imperial throne with the crown on his head, while from the high altar was intoning, "Lord God, we praise thee." Meanwhile the bells were ringing, cannons thundering, and the people loudly acclaiming.

Immediately after this solemnity the procession again formed, and escorted the emperor to the Römer Palace. The road was laid with cloth, embroidered with red, black, and gold, which, immediately after the procession had passed, was seized by the people and torn into a thousand pieces.

All this princely splendor of the declining German empire Louisa witnessed with great interest, as one can readily imagine.

A fact, although insignificant in appearance,

is worthy of attention, because it testifies to the simplicity and industry of the young princess. Louisa, when afterward queen, related that the shoes which she wore on the occasion of one of these coronations, which, in conformity with the fashion, must be of silk, were made by her own hands.

But much more than such display did Louisa enjoy the sight of the homely town life which she was permitted to look upon in the house of Frau Rath Goethe, the mother of the German poet. Here, on one occasion, she, with her brother, saw the old lady comfortably eating a bacon salad, with omelets, and it afforded the two great pleasure to be asked to join her at this meal. They did not leave the table until every morsel was eaten.

These short excursions, which Louisa made in her fourteenth and sixteenth years to Frankfort-on-the-Main, were followed by a journey to Hildburghausen to see her eldest sister, the wife of the reigning duke. She was accompanied by her grandmother and her younger sister Frederica. They found it necessary to make this journey on account of the war. Germany at this time was waging war against France, and the country along the Rhine was in great danger. Frankfort-on-the-Main was, in the course of a single week, in the possession of the French; the Prussians, however, pressed forward, and the French were obliged to give up the city.

Frederic William II. commanded a part of his troops in person. His sons, the Crown Prince Frederic William and Prince Louis, shared the dangers and glories of the war, as was always the custom with the Prussian princes.

Those who had taken refuge in Hildburghausen during the winter were able to return to Darmstadt in the spring. The Landgrave of Hesse, an ally of Frederic William II., wrote to the landgravine that she might return by way of Frankfort. Frederic William had chosen this city for his head-quarters, and Louisa and her sister were now permitted to be introduced to the king, to whom they were related. The wife of the king and the deceased mother of the princesses were cousins.

III.

Betrothal.

THE king was delighted to find in his young relatives so many excellent qualities. Louisa had grown tall and stately, and made, by her youthful beauty, as well as by her gentle and noble, yet plain and simple nature, a deep impression. Her clear blue eyes were the mirror wherein was reflected her pure spirit. In her disposition were blended a gentleness and nobility of soul seldom to be met with. They were manifested in every word and beamed in every glance. This blending of sweetness and gentleness with a certain exaltedness of character, one might almost say a moral pride, was the power whereby she influenced so deeply and permanently all who knew her.

The landgravine was expecting to leave the same evening for Darmstadt, but an invitation to dine with the king deferred the journey. On this occasion the Prussian princes were also present, and had the opportunity of becoming acquainted with the daughters of the Grand Duke of Mecklenburg-Strelitz. The Crown Prince Frederic William saw Louisa, and that first sight was decisive. " She is the one, or none other on earth," whispered a voice within to the prince, as he afterward confessed. Louisa had a similar premonition.

No political or family considerations had any influence here. This union was one of true affinity, and though it was not settled that evening, the preliminary steps were taken. For such a man as the prince, Louisa was the proper person.

"In later years," so relates Bishop Eylert, after death had dissolved the happy marriage, "the king remembered with especial pleasure the remarkable, and to him ever new and fresh, impression which Louisa made on him when he saw her for the first time in Frankfort. The moment of the new acquaintance was also the moment of mutual affection."

"We find," said the king, when speaking to the bishop of this mutual sympathy which unites congenial hearts, "in Schiller's writings some very beautiful lines, where it is excellently and truly shown how, at first sight, this mutual love is conceived. In our case it was no sentimental fancy, but a clearly-marked consciousness, which at the same time caused us both to weep. O God, what worlds lie between that first moment when I found her and this, wherein I deplore her loss! With pleasure I recall the past, and often wish to read those lines of Schiller again; but I cannot find them."

Eylert read the following lines of Schiller to the king :—

> " How it did chance, I ask myself in vain :—
> Whence she did come, and how she did discover

Herself to me, that ask I,—For as I
Did turn my eyes, I found her by my side;
And darkly powerful, wonderful, her presence
Laid hold on me, my very inmost being.
Her witching smile, so pure, it was not moved me;
The charms 'twas not, which on her cheeks so played,
Nor e'en the glance of her bright eye so pure:—
It was her deepest and most secret life
That moved in me such strong and holy power.
As force of spell incomprehensibly acts—
Our souls appeared, without the help of speech
Or any means, themselves to touch in spirit,
E'en as my breath did mingle there with hers;
Quite strange to me, and yet she only trusted,
And clear at once I felt it in me grow:
She is the one, or else none other on earth!
That is the love of holy heaven's beam,
Which in the soul doth deeply strike and burn
When it discovers affinities to affinities.
There can be no resistance and no choice;
Let man not loose what heaven itself hath bound!"

"Yes, yes," answered the king, after he had heard the words of the poet, "that is the piece, and I think it very beautiful. But it makes now quite another impression. The roses have fallen, and only the thorns remain. There is more in marriage than in poetry! The latter is to me now too sickening. I dare not give myself to it. It weakens one, and is not adapted to those duties which devolve upon me in these heavier and sterner times."

Prince Louis was attracted to Frederica in the same manner as his elder brother was to Louisa. The following month, on the 24th of April, 1793, the double betrothals were solemnized at Darmstadt. The king himself changed the rings between the affianced couples. The crown prince was twenty-three years old, Louisa a month before had completed her seventeenth year.

Two days afterward the princes returned with their father to the camp, leaving the two affianced brides in Darmstadt to wait until the war was over. At the end of May they visited with their grandmother the head-quarters of the king at Bodenheim, in order to have an interview with the princes.

In Goethe's account of the " Siege of Mayence," he gives a lively description of his visit

4

to the German camp at Bodenheim, where he saw the two princesses, Louisa and Frederica. He says, " I accompanied my most gracious sovereign to the left wing, and waited for the Landgrave of Darmstadt, whose camp was beautifully ornamented with branches of fir. The king's tent, however, exceeded any thing of the kind I have ever seen. It was comfortable, beautifully adorned, and really luxuriant. As evening approached a spectacle of remarkable interest was prepared for us.

" The princesses of Mecklenburg had dined at head-quarters in Bodenheim with his majesty the king, and now were making an informal visit to the camp. I stepped quietly back into my tent, and could carefully observe these princely ladies, who promenaded immediately before my tent. And I must say, that, in the midst of the havoc and din of war, these two ladies seemed to me to be apparitions from heaven, and they made upon me an impression never to be effaced."

IV.

As Crown Princess.

THE King of Prussia was very much opposed to the tardy campaign. He had commenced the war in the thought and hope, as he had before expressed it to the widow of Frederic the Great, to quench the frightful outbreak of anarchy, which desolated France, and would soon have overrun the whole continent. To accomplish this purpose he summoned his whole might, and showed genuine Prussian zeal and courage in declaring war against the Revolution. His sons gave repeated proofs of their bravery and intrepidity. Thus, at the bombardment of Verdun, as the king and the crown prince, who were on horseback, remained in the midst of the Prussian artillery, a ball struck the ground only a few paces from them.

" Your majesty exposes yourself too much," said the prince.

" Frederic exposed himself still more at Kunersdorf," answered the king, and rode on with the crown prince; but on the other side of a battery he added, " Truly it would be a triumph to the enemy if they could· say they had shot the King of Prussia after they had taken prisoner the French king."

They had gone, however, but a few steps further before they saw another cannon-ball strike still nearer to them.

" Sire, I beg you, let me remain here alone!" said the crown prince.

" No," answered the king, " I shall remain here to be a witness of your coolness."

Also, when Frankfort was taken by storm under the Prussian General Rüchel, the king and the crown prince were in the midst of a fierce cannonade.

The greatest danger, however, befel Prince Louis. Wearied by duty, he had thrown himself down on his couch in his own room near to the fire-place, in which a bright fire burned. He fell asleep, and while thus unconscious the couch caught fire, and was soon in a flame. His clothes were already burning, when a sentry rushed in and saved him from a horrible death. Every thing he had became a prey to the flames. The crown prince then made it the subject of a joke, and made a collection from the queen and her followers "for the poor burnt-out man."

As a counterpart to this rescue of Prince Louis by the Pomeranian dragoon may be mentioned the fearlessness with which Prince Louis Ferdinand, in the same campaign, carried an Austrian soldier from under the hostile musket-fire. It occurred on the 14th of July, 1793, when the prince and an Austrian regiment were repulsed by the enemy. A soldier belonging to that regiment, having received a wound in his shoulder, sank to the ground from weakness. None of his comrades, however, dare go to his aid, for fear of falling into the hands of the enemy. Not even the reward which the prince offered to any one who would save the poor helpless man induced any of them to expose his life.

" If none of you will take pity upon a poor comrade, I will show you what a soldier's duty is," said the prince, and he rushed to the wounded man, and brought him back to the regiment unhurt by the fire of the enemy, who now aimed directly at him. This deed made Prince Louis Ferdinand very much beloved by the army, and even with the Austrians he was a great favorite, so much so that they offered him high promotion if he would fight under the imperial flag. But he answered that it only became a Prussian prince to fight under Prussian colors.

The last battle which the Prussians fought in this campaign under the eye of their sovereign was that at Pirmasens, from whose heights they drove the French triumphantly.

The enemy left on the field four thousand dead, two thousand prisoners, and ninety-eight cannon.

Notwithstanding such bravery and successful feats of arms, it did not go well with the united German armies. In proportion as they, in the commencement, made great advancement, so afterward did they make slow progress. The Duke of Brunswick, at the time of the storming of Frankfort, was at variance with General Rüchel. The king had given the latter the order to attack; but while he was preparing to lead his columns forward, the Duke, by a counter order, stopped the movement, and would hear nothing of an attack on the city. This one event marked the whole course of the war. Under such circumstances it is not surprising that the king lost all interest in the campaign. In September he returned to Berlin, and soon his sons followed him thither.

Nothing now prevented the marriage of the betrothed ones. The two princes, Frederic

William and Louis Ferdinand, started homeward at the close of November, visiting their
affianced on their journey, and arriving in Berlin on the 8th of December, 1793.

Eight days later, Louisa, with her sister
Frederica, departed from Darmstadt, in order
to go to the capital of the kingdom, whose
queen she was in future to be. On their route
they visited Wurzburg, Hildburghausen, Weimar, Leipzig, and Wittenberg, arriving at Potsdam on the 21st of December. On the following day, the 22d, they made their entrance into
Berlin. It was a day of universal rejoicing in
that great capital. Very early in the morning,
throngs of people could be seen in the streets.
It seemed as if all Berlin were going out of the
Brandenburg gate to meet the princess, of
whose rare beauty and amiability all had heard.
The crown prince and Prince Louis, who on
the 20th had gone to meet the affianced brides,
had returned, and were waiting to receive them
at the royal palace in Berlin.

In Schönberg, a village about half a mile
from the city, on the road to Potsdam, the
guilds and corporation of Berlin were stationed
to escort the State carriage into the city. The
order for the procession had been previously
arranged with great minuteness. The etiquette
for such occasions demanded that the carriage
of an arriving princess should always be preceded by one containing several chamberlains,
in order that they might be able to receive her
immediately on descending from her carriage.
This mode of procedure was to have been observed on this day ; but some of the citizens
objected to the arrangement, because it seemed
as though they were escorting the chamberlains, and they insisted that the carriage of the
princess should come first; "for," said they,
"we go out to meet the princess, and not the
chamberlains." The Court-marshal, after much
hesitation, yielded to the citizens. A great
multitude had gone out to Schönberg, that
they might, as soon as possible, get a glance at

the future queen ; they then accompanied the
procession, which took its way slowly through
the Brandenburg gate, and then along Leipsig-
street and William-street to Linden-street,
amid continuous huzzaing. The end of Linden-street, where the monument of Frederic
the Great stands, with the royal palace on
the one side and the university buildings on
the other, was the central point of attraction.
There was a great triumphal arch built, richly
adorned with symbolical pictures, after the
manner of those erected in olden time to do
honor to returning victorious warriors.

At this place were assembled a large group
of children, for the purpose of welcoming and
congratulating the lovely princess. On the
one side stood the boys, and on the other side
the girls ; the latter were dressed in white, and
their heads adorned with wreaths. They had
prepared a poem of welcome for Louisa, in
which they said that the Prussian people had
feared, when the crown prince went forth to

the war, that he might be defeated, but now they were rejoiced to see him return as *conqueror* and *conquered* — conqueror over the French, and conquered by the most charming of princesses. A lovely little girl, who so beautifully recited the verses, so charmed the princess by her sweetness, that she stooped down and drew the child to the carriage window and kissed her several times, much to the chagrin and horror of the Countess Von Voss, the lady in waiting, who sat with Louisa in the carriage, and who declared this spontaneous action contrary to all rules of court etiquette. She exclaimed :

"What has your Royal Highness done? That is exceedingly improper !"

"What !" answered Louisa simply ; "am I allowed to do this no more ?"

The people were rejoiced at this incident, which so beautifully gave them a glimpse of her disposition. They felt that she would not only be the *queen*, but the *mother* of her people. Every tongue was burdened with her praise.

The kindness with which she received the first present in the city which in future was to be her home, the thoughtful words of gratitude that she gave to those who presented it, and the amiableness of disposition of which her every act testified, laid the first stone of that monument which she afterward built for herself in the hearts of the Prussians.

From the triumphal arch the procession proceeded to the royal palace, where Louisa, with her sister, was received by the royal family and the two princes. On Christmas Eve the marriage of the crown prince and Louisa was celebrated with great pomp and magnificence, the diamond crown of the house of Prussia being placed on her fair brow. The royal pair were united according to the forms of their faith in the brilliantly illuminated white saloon. Kneeling on an elegant cushion, under a canopy of crimson velvet, surmounted by two crowns, Bishop Sack pronounced the benediction. The booming of seventy-two cannon announced that the ceremony was over.

After the family had partaken of the banquet which had been so elaborately prepared for them, under a covering made of crimson velvet embroidered with gold, they returned to the saloon, where they joined in the dance, each bearing a lighted torch, according to the custom of the Middle Ages. Eighteen State ministers joined the procession, and marched slowly and solemnly to the sound of the music.

The citizens of Berlin wished to celebrate this great occasion by a general illumination of the city. The crown prince told them that it would please him far better if they would use the money which it would cost for an illumination for the benefit of the widows and orphans of those who had fallen in the war. It was done, and the members of the royal family each contributed toward the fund, so that many a poor family was made happy, and spent a merrier Christmas than they otherwise could have done.

In order that as many of the citizens as practicable might enjoy the festivities of the royal household, the king commanded that a large number of tickets should be distributed. These were given, however, to a great extent, to the officers of the royal household, who appeared in their uniforms. When the old king saw how few persons clothed as citizens were present, he was very much irritated at the improper fulfillment of his commands.

" Do you not see enough embroidered collars about you ? " he muttered. " I wish to see the holiday dresses of civilians also. The day after to-morrow, at the second wedding, (that of Prince Louis and Princess Frederica,) let no tickets be given out, but admit all who have on a proper coat."

This command, which was precisely obeyed, caused the apartments of the palace to be filled with spectators from all stations in life.

The crowd was so great that it was very difficult for any one to pass about. The king himself, who was a large, corpulent man, could not make any progress, not even with the aid of the people, who tried to make room for him. After many vain attempts he bethought himself, and, instead of going directly forward, he turned himself and went sidewise, with his right elbow in advance. Then he said to the crowd pleasantly:

"Don't inconvenience yourselves, children. The bridegroom's father must not allow himself to-day more space than the bridal pair."

On Christmas Day the crown prince and Louisa went first to the royal cathedral, and from thence to their beautiful but plain palace, where Frederic William, as crown prince and as king, lived all his life.

V.

Domestic Life.

THE married and domestic life of the newly-married pair was established in the fear of God, simplicity of heart, purity of purpose, and true love, and this was to the whole land a worthy example of German home-life. A happier or more perfect bond than this could not exist—a bond of two noble and congenial hearts, though varying in talents and disposition.

The crown prince was said to be the handsomest man in Prussia. He was tall and finely proportioned, with a military bearing, a calm brow, dark blue eyes, and an open, intellectual countenance. He was very earnest, and appeared to some reserved and morose. He talked but little, and then usually in short sentences, and explained his meaning in few, but intelligible words. With his earnestness he united great mildness of nature, and was so willing and condescending, and, above all, so conscientious, that he made a lasting impression on those with whom he came in contact. Louisa was tall and slender, with a face that combined great beauty of feature with a very sweet expression. Her manner was elegant and dignified, her voice clear and musical, her conversation brilliant and engaging. She possessed a joyous disposition, which had not been suppressed in her youth, but, on the contrary, had been developed and unfolded by her free, unrestrained education. She was always happy, and knew well how to cheer and encourage her husband when oppressed with the cares of the world. She was, indeed, a help-meet, and became indispensable to him.

It was the custom in those times for husbands and wives to address each other as "you," (sie,) instead of "thou," (du,) after the

5

French custom. The crown prince and Louisa did not adhere to this custom, and used the familiar term "thou."

They never felt at home at court—nowhere but in their own little palace. When they returned to this loved home from the festivities of the court, the crown prince, with beaming countenance, would take his wife's hand, and exclaim :

"Thank God, thou art once more my wife !"

And when Louisa would say :

"And am I not, then, always thy wife ?"

He would reply, with a half-comical sigh,

" Ah, no! thou too often art only the crown princess !"

The confidential manner of the prince and princess, with their unembarrassed deportment, which was in violation of all usages of court etiquette, was to Countess Von Voss, the lady in waiting, a matter of serious discomfiture. She sought every opportunity to make improvements in the royal household, but with little success. She was especially annoyed to know that the crown prince entered his wife's apartments without being duly announced.

"Very good," said the prince one day, as the lady of ceremonies was favoring him with a lecture on the influence of etiquette on the future history of the world, " I will submit, and in order to show you that I mean what I say, I beg to ask if I can have the honor of speaking to my consort, Her Royal Highness, the Crown Princess ?"

Who could be happier than this mistress of ceremonies when she saw the honor of the court preserved ? With a solemn mien she went to the apartment of the crown princess to beg an audience for her husband, the crown prince. What was her astonishment when, on entering the room of Louisa, she saw the crown prince sitting by her side on the sofa !

"See!" exclaimed he, smiling, "dear countess,

my wife and I see and speak to each other as often as we like, *unannounced*, and thus it is in all honorable meetings. You are a charming lady of ceremonies, but we are a pair of good Christian people."

On another occasion a similar deception was played upon the Countess Von Voss. She had arranged that, at a certain court ceremonial, the crown prince and princess should ride in a carriage with six span of horses, and attended by two coachmen and three footmen in elegant liveries. He listened to the lady's reasons for so grandly arranging every thing for their comfort and pleasure, but at the same time planning a proceeding more to his own liking. At the appointed hour the carriages came to the door of the palace. The prince assisted the countess into the one he designed for her, closed the door, and ordered the coachman to drive on. He had provided for himself and Louisa an open carriage, with only two pair of horses. This arrangement was much more pleasing to the royal pair than the one the countess had proposed.

This royal household was more like that of a private citizen than that of a prince. Both Frederic William and Louisa had been trained to contentment from their childhood, and in this respect were well adapted to each other. Neither of them had the slightest desire for display. At a later period, when king, Frederic William said to his newly-married son, for whom he had arranged a princely mansion,

"I had not so grand a palace when I married your mother. I only hope that you may be as happy and contented as we were."

On the 10th of March, 1794, Louisa celebrated her eighteenth birthday in Berlin, the first after her marriage. It was for her a day of much joy. The court and the city vied with each other in doing her honor. The king presented to her, as a summer residence, the chateau of Oranienburg, which, for a long time uninhabited, had been restored and magnificently furnished.   As a proof of Louisa's goodness of heart, on this day she thought of the poor and needy.   She asked the king if he would grant her one more wish, and that wish was that she might have "a handful of gold to distribute among the poor of Berlin," that they might share with her the joy of the day.

The king answered, smiling, that it depended upon how much she considered a handful.

She quickly replied, for she never was at a loss for an answer:

"As large as the heart of the best of kings."

And the poor had abundant cause to be thankful to Louisa, who all her life lost no opportunity of doing them kindnesses.

In celebration of this day the crown princess, together with her sister, gave a feast to their servants.   Each person was allowed to invite several guests, and when they came to be seated at the table, eighty individuals were counted.   Louisa complained that the hundred was not completed.

She extended the same kindness to the unknown children that she met in the castle gardens. She took them up, and lovingly embraced them. Once, as a strange little boy ran into her arms, Louisa quieted the indignation of the court ladies by saying :

" Let him alone ; a boy must be wild."

Then tapping the child on the cheek, she said in a friendly tone :

" Run now, my little fellow, and carry a greeting from me to your parents."

She treated the mothers of these children that she met in her rambles in the same friendly manner. The salutations of her subjects she always returned with great kindness.

Immediately after her coronation she wrote the following to her grandmother :

" I am queen, and what rejoices me most is the hope that I shall not find it necessary to count my benefactions."

She was not satisfied merely to relieve the necessity of the moment, but she sought out the cause of the poverty, and prevented it by giving employment to the unfortunate. If she discovered that the poor owed their necessity to themselves, she did not cease to sympathize, but said :

" We ought not to inquire whether the poor deserve help. Who can weigh and determine that ?   And in what do we deserve the goodness of God ?   Is he not all pity and grace ? "

Louisa resided at the chateau of Oranienburg during the summers of 1794 and 1795. Her first son, Frederic William IV., who afterward became king, was born there on the 15th of October, 1795, and her second son, William I., the present king, on the 22d of March, 1797.

Besides these two sons, she had five other children : a daughter, Charlotte, born on the 13th of July, 1798, who was afterward married to the Emperor Nicholas of Russia ; Prince Charles, born on the 29th of June, 1801 ; Alexandrine, born on the 23d of February,

1803, afterward Grand Duchess of Mecklen-burg-Schwerin ; Louisa, born on the 21st of February, 1808, wife of Prince Frederic of the Netherlands ; and last, Prince Albert, born on the 4th of October, 1809.

Louisa brought up her children in the fear of God, and cultivated in them loving-kindness, patriotism, and a disposition for all that was noble, good, and holy. The very remarkable influence which the queen exercised over her "treasures," as she called them, will be seen hereafter.

We have already shown how repulsive the formalities of court etiquette were to this happy pair, and the chagrin of the lady of ceremonies at their undignified behavior.

We relate another amusing incident, to illustrate the playfulness of Louisa's disposition.

One warm summer day, in the year 1795, while at the chateau of Oranienburg, Louisa informed Countess Von Voss that the crown prince and herself had decided to take a drive into the woods, and would be pleased to have her accompany them. She replied that it would give her great pleasure, and hastened to join them. But what was her surprise on arriving at the door to see the royal pair in a rough wagon, to which a pair of large, awkward horses were yoked, and without a footman. Louisa repeated her invitation, and in vain the crown prince joined his persuasion to hers.

The punctilious countess was not to be moved to participate in *such* pleasure. Without saying a word, she went back into the castle, and the happy pair made their rural excursion alone, highly enjoying the joke which they had had at the expense of the countess.

Frederic William and Louisa were once standing at an open window of the castle in Potsdam after they had become king and queen. Louisa was holding one of her children in her arms, and allowing it to play with a small gold piece. An old man, scantily

though cleanly dressed, approached the window. He bowed to the king and queen, not knowing who they were.

"Please help, good sir, a poor man who has been disowned by his undutiful daughters. My only son is a soldier, and is now on the frontier."

The king answered him graciously, without further question:

"Ask this lady, my friend. You see she allows her child to play with gold pieces, and she will probably have something left for a poor old man who has been deserted by his children. I have not my purse with me."

The queen gave the little prince four Frederic's d'or ($14 40) in his hand, and said to him,

"Give them to the man."

The prince threw them gladly into the hat of the old man, who was quite amazed at receiving so much, and turned away from the window with tears in his eyes.

He had scarcely gone ten steps when the queen called after him :

" Friend, please return again."

The old man returned.

" What is your name, my friend ? " asked the queen.

" Berghof," he answered. " I was formerly a saddler in Brandenburg ; for twenty-three years I served Frederic the Great, and was discharged as sergeant."

" Without a pension ? " asked the queen.

And his answer was,

" Yes, madam."

" This gentleman," said she, pointing to the king, " says he has not his purse with him ; but he has pen, ink, and paper, and his handwriting is as good as gold."

The king, moved by this good-natured as well as *naïve* sally of his sweet wife, went from the window, seated himself at his writing-desk, and soon returned with a small slip of paper, on which were written these words :

" Old Berghof of Brandenburg is to receive a pension of twelve thalers ($8 64) monthly from the extraordinary treasury of war.

"FREDERIC WILLIAM."
"TO THE WAR TREASURY IN BERLIN."

Now, for the first time, was Berghof aware that he had been addressing the king and queen. He wished to give expression to his gratitude in the most sincere and heartfelt manner possible; but the king did not wait for this scene. He closed the window and went quickly away, leaving the old man alone in his joyful and extraordinary astonishment.

VI.

In Paretz.

THE chateau of Oranienburg was far too magnificent for persons of such taste as Frederic William and Louisa. They often sighed for a quiet home, in which they could live without restraint. The crown prince, therefore, purchased the estate of Paretz, where every thing was ordered simply and plainly, yet comfortably. There was no expensive furniture, no splendidly adorned walls, no curtains of velvet and damask, no gold table-service, nor expensive works of art. The grounds even owed their beauty to nature more than art. Every thing was arranged with great simplicity. The prince used to say to the architect, "Always bear in mind that you are building for a poor proprietor."

Many happy days were passed at Paretz, even after Frederic William had become king. One day, when a foreign princess asked Louisa if she did not often feel lonely in that hermitage, she received the following reply:

"Oh no, I am quite happy in being the worthy 'Lady of Paretz.'"

And her husband, after being crowned king, wished to be regarded by his family and the neighborhood only as the "Proprietor of Paretz."

There they enjoyed the pleasures of real country life; they hunted, took excursions on the water, and joined in the feasts that attend harvest-time and church-consecrations. Louisa often forgot her "highness-ship," and, along with her husband, mixed with the young peasantry in their festivities. Equally pleasant was it to her, on the occasion of the yearly fairs at Paretz, to go to the booths and buy little baskets of cake and confectionery, and distribute them among old and young.

On one occasion she gave to all the children of the village new clothes for the harvest festival. When the little girls and boys came in procession to the castle to thank her, she felt as happy as if she had received the richest present herself, and she said to her husband, "Except ye become as little children!"

In this beautiful retreat the heart of the princess was full of joy. "What can give greater happiness," she said, "than, divested of one's external greatness, to go, in true nobleness of heart, and rejoice with the joyful and sorrow with the sorrowful?"

An intense love of nature was *one* of her chief characteristics through life. "Amid the quiet and beauty of nature," as she expressed it, "she could best rally and collect her mind, whose chords, like those of an instrument of music, which needed each day to be drawn up in order to get the right tone." "If I neglect that," she said, "I feel out of harmony, which, by the din of the world, is made worse.

What blessings lie around us that we know /
nothing of!"

A welcome and frequent visitor at Paretz
was General von Kockeritz, the adjutant of the
crown prince. This faithful general, who was
a great favorite at the palace, was, later, constantly in attendance upon Frederic William
when king. Louisa was sorry to notice that
when dinner was finished the general always
seemed in haste to depart. She asked the
crown prince why it was that he did so, and
received the following reply:

" Let the old man alone; he must have his
domestic comfort after dinner."

Louisa was not satisfied with this answer,
and inquired further, and soon learned what it
was that took the general so hastily from the
table.

One day, as he arose to leave in his usual
haste, Louisa immediately went to him with a
pipe in one hand, and a lighted taper in the
other, saying:

6

" No, good general, to-day you must not run away, but stay and smoke your accustomed pipe with us."

She put the pipe in the hand of the general, and related to her husband how she had long tried to find out the cause of his hasty retreat from the table. So the old general remained and smoked his pipe.

This act of kindness delighted the crown prince, and he said to his wife,

" Dear Louisa, you did that charmingly."

Not far from Paretz there lies, in the river Havel, Peacock Island. The family often made excursions there in summer. Once, after the crown prince and Louisa had become king and queen, after having dined beneath the shade of some pleasant beech-trees, they engaged in conversation, their children in the meanwhile wandering away from them. Suddenly the queen exclaimed,

" Where are the children ? "

She was told that they were playing in the

meadow of a young farmer. Then she said to the king :

" Can we not surprise them there ? "

The king answered that they might, but that they must go some distance around in the boat in order not to be perceived.

The king rowed while the queen stood up to search for them.

" Softly, softly," she remarked to the king.

The surprise was successful. Unnoticed, they stepped on shore, and the astonished children sprang toward them, shouting for joy.

On this same beautiful island there occurred another pleasant incident, which, although it belongs to a later period, we will relate it here. As the king and queen were sitting one calm summer evening under the shade of the magnificent oaks on Peacock Island, they requested Bishop Eylert, who was with them, to read a sermon that he had recently preached on Christian marriage. The text was from the beautiful words of Ruth to Naomi : " Entreat

me not to leave thee, or to return from following after thee : for whither thou goest, I will
go ; where thou lodgest, I will lodge : thy people
shall be my people, and thy God my God :
where thou diest, will I die, and there will I be
buried : the Lord do so to thee, and more also,
if aught but death part thee and me."

When he had finished, a holy calm seemed
to pervade the atmosphere around. Soon the
stillness was broken, and distant music was
heard echoing through the air, which came
from a military band. It was the beautiful
hymn, " In all my actions I take counsel of the
Lord." There was a deep silence, and Bishop
Eylert describes the scene as one of enchant-
ment.

" The moon had arisen, and was throwing
her soft light through the trees. It seemed to
us as if this lovely island were the temple of
the living God."

The king was the first to break the solemn
silence. He rose, and laying his hand on

Louisa's shoulder, said with great tenderness, and a heart full of emotion :

"This is my intention, dear Louisa—I and my house, we will serve the Lord."

He then left the company, and was very deeply affected. He then went down to the river, where he was hidden by a small thicket, and could meditate alone.

Louisa, differently from the king, had need of more open communication. She then spoke to the bishop of the gratitude of her heart, and said :

"Only in faith can I find support. In the longing after happiness I become sensible of a deep emptiness in my heart, which nothing earthly can satisfy. I can only find peace in looking to the Saviour. I have an unspeakable love for him. The highest and purest ideal of life and action is in him. One prays to him, and immediately feels drawn nearer his presence ; his eternal, self-sacrificing love has a gentle and wonderfully winning power.

" What elevates me most, and gives me the most happiness, is the thought that the king and I fully accord in our religious convictions. Through him I have become better.   I believe he is the best man and Christian on earth. Did you hear, as you finished reading your sermon, how he said with heartfelt emotion, ' This is my intention—I and my house, we will serve the Lord ?'   I wonder where he is, my best friend !   Come and let us seek him."

VII.

The Young Queen.

THREE deaths, following one after another, threw the royal family into deep sorrow. On the 28th of December, 1796, Prince Louis died of malignant fever, at the age of twenty-two years. On the 13th of January, 1797, Elizabeth Christine, widow of Frederic the Great, died. She had reached the advanced age of eighty-two years. She was distinguished for her kindness to the poor, and was greatly venerated by Louisa. When King Frederic William II. heard the news of her death, he remarked to a friend that he would soon follow her. His sickness increased and his strength diminished until the 16th of November, 1797, when he died.

The crown prince now ascended the throne

as Frederic William III. He and Louisa now, as king and queen, contented themselves with the same palace in which they had spent the first part of their married life. It had become dear to them, and therefore they continued to live in it in their simple and unostentatious manner. The whole country looked with pride upon their new king and queen, who were distinguished for so many virtues ; and this love of the people was to Louisa and Frederic William one of their chief sources of happiness.

The king and queen were often seen walking together without any attendants, save the people, who followed them with acclamations. At one time, when they were visiting the Christmas fair, they made purchases at the different booths. A woman, who was buying something, stopped on perceiving them, and stepped back. Louisa bade her remain, and asked kindly after her family. The woman told her that she had a son about the age of the crown prince. The queen immediately purchased a beautiful toy, and, presenting it to her, said :

" Give this to your 'crown prince' in the name of *mine.*"

We have a striking example of Louisa's kindness to a laborer. A count and the court-shoemaker were announced at the same time. She gave audience to the latter first, saying :

" The mechanic's time is far more valuable than the count's, and if I kept him waiting an hour or two, where would be the honor of being court-shoemaker ? The tradesman must be attended to first, and the count must wait."

Once, at a court entertainment, the queen observed that a beautiful lady was avoided by the nobility because she was not of noble blood, whereupon she asked the king to show her particular attention, which he did.

On another occasion, at a presentation in Magdeburg, an officer's wife was asked concerning her birth, whether she was of noble family. When the lady, deeply embarrassed, answered that she was of "common origin," the queen was moved to pity at seeing her great confusion, amid the contemptuous smiles of those standing near. Louisa leaned toward her kindly, and spoke, in a tone loud enough for all to hear, of her worthy family and really deserving ancestry; "but," continued she, "goodness is not confined to any station in life; it blossoms amid the low as well as the high. Inner personal goodness, after all, is the only true nobleness."

At a grand Church festival at Potsdam a poor woman inadvertently took the queen's seat, and was turned out in a very rude manner by the master of ceremonies. Louisa was very much annoyed at his harshness, and would not be satisfied until she had seen and made recompense to the woman.

One fine spring morning, as the queen was taking a walk in the castle garden at Potsdam, she saw a sick man sitting on a bench. As he seemed, from his clothing, to be poor, she ordered her servants to give him ten dollars. The man was the master-mason of Potsdam, who had been very ill, which accounted for his poverty-stricken appearance. Not being in want, he honorably declined the gift. When the queen heard of this she returned, for she had gone some distance. Fearing she had offended the man by her proffered alms, she said :

" I hope that you will pardon me if I have given offense. I did not intend it."

She then asked him if he would allow her cook to superintend his food until he was well again. He complied with her wish, and went each day, for several weeks, at midday to the royal palace, where the most nourishing food was prepared for him.

The never-ceasing benevolence of the queen caused often her quarterly allowance of money to be exhausted. She once asked the treasurer, Wolter, who was a very accurate and trustworthy man, to let her have money in advance.

He told her that he could not do that ; his duty was to pay all at the *proper* time ; and until it was due he dare not advance any thing, the king would not allow it. "Besides, your majesty," continued he, "if I were to do so, you would still run short."

"Good Wolter," the queen replied, "I love my children, and the term 'child of the country' has a sweet sound to me ; nothing gives me so much joy as, by the side of my husband, the 'father of the country,' to be 'mother of the country.' I must and dare not fail in my duty, and, above all, I must help where there is need."

"All right," answered Wolter, "I'll tell that to the king."

"But not so," replied Louisa, "as to offend him."

The king, who was of like mind, was not offended.

Soon after Louisa found her money-box full, and she asked,

"What angel has filled that box again ?"

"The angels are legion," replied the king.

It is worthy of remark that the king remained plain and simple in his habits. On the day of his ascension to the throne a servant threw open for him both of the folding doors.

"Have I then become stout so suddenly," asked he, "that one door is too narrow for me ?"

And when the cook had supplied the royal table with two more dishes than were formerly placed on his table as crown prince, he remarked that they seemed to think, since yesterday, he had become possessed of a greater appetite.

On the occasion of the first banquet after his coronation, the king told the court-marshal, who stood behind his chair, to sit down to table.

"I dare not," was the answer, "until your majesty has taken your first glass."

Such had been the command of the ceremony-loving Louis XIV.

"Is any particular drink required by etiquette?" asked Frederic William.

"So far as I know, no, sire," was the reply.

Then the king took a glass of water, and drank, saying:

"Now you can take your seat, for I have drank."

The king, in the commencement of his reign, could be approached by all. Once a fisher-woman came from Schwedt, and related to him that Prince Louis, shortly before his death, had promised her husband six thousand thalers to build a new house. Fifteen hundred thalers had already been paid, but now both the prince and her husband were dead, and she was a poor, helpless widow. She told him that she had heard that Prince Louis' brother had become king, and that was the reason she came to Berlin. She concluded by saying:

"Your brother was a generous man, and I hope you will be, and let me have my house built."

The king gave directions that the money should be paid to her in Schwedt.

The thankful woman left, but soon returned to Berlin, bringing to the king a small cask of lampreys.

"Now, I see," she said, "that you are as good and liberal a man as your brother, and I have brought you something for your kindness."

The king took the present, and gave it to Louisa.

The following pleasing incident is another evidence of Louisa's unwearied efforts to make others happy. There was an old man living in Darmstadt, who, in former years, had been the teacher of Louisa. He had been very much attached to his pupil, and she to him. As he was continually hearing of her goodness and benevolence, and of her thoughtfulness for poor as well as rich, he conceived a greater desire than ever to see her once more. This thought occupied his mind continually, until at last he determined to make the journey to Berlin. In those days a journey to Berlin from Darmstadt was no light undertaking, especially to an old man. The old teacher, being in comfortable circumstances, could afford the expense of the journey; he therefore packed his trunk, and started by the post-coach for Berlin. As he journeyed on, day after day and night after night, he wondered whether the queen would recognize him, and how she would receive him. At length he arrived at his destination, and took rooms at a plain hotel.

The following morning he put on his best coat, and went up to the palace. He passed the sentinel, and entered the great hall. Ladies and gentlemen in elegant costumes passed by him without a word, or even a look. He felt embarrassed and frightened, but still went on. He finally came to the ante-chamber, and there saw an attendant, and asked him if he would please announce him to the queen. The attendant inquired what name he should give.

He was requested to say, "An old acquaintance from Darmstadt wishes to speak to her majesty." The man in waiting soon returned, and ushered the old teacher into the presence of the queen.

She was sitting on a sofa, but no sooner saw him than she recognized him, and stepped toward him, calling him by name. The old man was deeply moved, and the queen's eyes were also suffused with tears as she pressed his hand. He then told her how often he had heard her spoken of as being a good queen, and kind and friendly to the poor, and for that reason he wished to see his old pupil once more before he died. She replied that she had many times thought of him, and was glad to have an opportunity of thanking him for the patience he had shown in instructing her, and of rewarding him for his labor. He quickly

7

said that he wished no reward, as he was in very comfortable circumstances.

The king now entered, and the queen introduced her former teacher to him. Frederic William was pleased to see him, and kindly took his hand. While they were conversing dinner was announced, and the king invited the worthy teacher to dine with him. The old teacher was terrified at this, and excused himself. They urged him, however, until he consented. His heart throbbed as he entered the stately dining-room, and was seated at the royal table, where he saw such dazzling and expensive service. The guests looked at the plainly-dressed, gray-headed old man in mute astonishment; but when the queen introduced him as her former teacher, then all had a kindly word for him. It was with great difficulty that the old man prevented the tears from running down his cheeks. Louisa, to relieve him of embarrassment, repeated amusing anecdotes of her youth, causing every one to laugh, and at the

Louisa and her Old Teacher

same time drawing her old friend into conversation. He afterward spoke of this hour spent at the table of the king as one of the happiest in his life.

After dinner he was escorted back to the queen's apartments, where Louisa, in the presence of her husband, presented him with a miniature portrait of herself, set with diamonds, at the same time saying that, if he would not accept money, he must accept from her a souvenir of his visit to Berlin. The king also said to him that so long as he remained in the city he should consider him as his guest, and that he had ordered an adjutant to be in attendance upon him, and show him all the objects of interest in Berlin. The next morning a carriage was at the door ready to conduct him about the city.

During his stay he saw every thing of interest in and around Berlin. The best of every thing was served to him at the hotel table, and when he complained of such luxuries, he was told that it was at the king's command.

When the time for his departure came, and he wished to settle his account with the landlord of the hotel, he was not allowed to pay any thing, as he had been the king's guest. An extra coach was provided at the royal command to convey him to Darmstadt. He visited the palace once more to bid the king and queen farewell, and to thank them for their kindness. Happy, indeed, was that old man as he journeyed home in the remembrance of that delightful and never-to-be-forgotten visit, and in the possession of that costly token of the queen's gratitude.

The following is a striking illustration of Louisa's thoughtfulness in behalf of a suffering prisoner :

In a cleft of a mountain range in Upper Silesia, through which the wild and raging river Neisse forces its passage down to the Oder, stands the Prussian fortress of Glatz, a natural fastness, begirt by mountain peaks like walls, and fortified yet more by human skill. The valley itself is shut out from the rest of the world, and inclosed by the massive walls and gratings of the castle. Woe to the man imprisoned in Glatz! Every thing calls out to him, "No hope remains for thee! no hope!"

Here, in the early part of this century, lay the Count of M., hopelessly shut in behind bolts and bars. By treason against the realm, and especially by personal violence offered to Frederick William III. of Prussia, he had invoked the anger of that monarch on his head, and was condemned to solitary imprisonment for life.

For a whole year he lay in his frightful, lonely cell without one ray of hope, either as to this world or the next,—for he was a skeptic. They had left him only one book—a Bible—and this for a long time he would not read ; or, if forced to take it up to relieve his weariness, it was only read with a feeling of hatred toward the God it reveals.

But sore affliction, that has brought back to the Good Shepherd many a wandering sheep, had a good effect upon the Count of M. The more he read his Bible the more he felt its influence on his forlorn and hopeless heart.

On a rough and stormy November night, when the mountain gales howled round the fortress, the rain fell in torrents, and the swollen and foaming Neisse rushed furiously down the valley, the count lay sleepless on his cot. The tempest in his breast was as fearful as that without. His whole past life arose before him; he was convicted of his manifold short-comings and sins; he felt that the source of all his misery lay *in his forsaking God.* For the first time in his life his heart was tender, and his eyes wept tears of genuine repentance. He rose from his cot, opened his Bible, and his eyes fell on Psalm l, 15: "Call upon me in the day of trouble: I will deliver thee, and thou shalt glorify me." This word of God reached the depths of his soul. He fell on his knees for the first time since he was a child, and cried to God for mercy; and that gracious and compassionate God, who turns not away from the first impulse of faith toward him, heard the cry of this sufferer in the dungeon, and gave him a twofold deliverance.

The same night, in his palace at Berlin, King Frederic William III. lay sleepless in bed. Severe bodily pains tormented him, and in his utter exhaustion he begged of God to grant him a single hour of refreshing sleep. The favor was granted; and when he woke again he said to his wife, the good-hearted Louisa:

"God has looked upon me very graciously, and I may well be thankful to him. Who in my kingdom has wronged me most? I will forgive him."

"The Count of M.," replied Louisa, "who is imprisoned in Glatz."

"You are right," said the sick king; "let him be pardoned."

Day had not dawned over Berlin ere a courier was dispatched to Silesia, bearing to the prisoner in Glatz pardon and release.

VIII.

Louisa and her Subjects.

N the year following the ascension to the throne, the queen accompanied her husband on a visit he made to several of his provinces. This journey awakened much love among the people toward their new king and queen, and especially did the latter win even a still higher place in their hearts. There are a *few* old people still living who remember this visit, and recall the impression the queen made ; but more than all can they remember the continuous festivity which that visit made.

Before setting out on this journey the king gave directions that no show or display should be made in their homes, saying, in his pithy manner, that the love of his people did him more honor than any triumphal arches, ceremonious receptions, and poetical effusions could do. Notwithstanding the king's orders, the royal pair every-where met with demonstrations of love and joy.

The journey was first through the provinces of Pomerania and Prussia, to Königsberg. At Stargard, in Pomerania, where a vast multitude had assembled to welcome them, nineteen little girls went in advance and strewed their way with flowers. Louisa conversed like a mother with the children, whereupon they gained confidence in her, and told her that there would have been twenty of them had not one been sent home, "*because she was not pretty enough.*"

"The poor child," said the queen, "she has rejoiced over our coming, and now she must weep bitterly at home."

She sent immediately for this child, and when she came the queen singled her out as the object of her particular attention.

In the village of Kaslin a crowd of peasants surrounded the carriage, and the *chief* man of

the place stepped up and asked in German if
the queen would alight for a moment, as the
people wanted to give her a "*treat.*" She accordingly descended from the carriage and
entered a cottage, where she found an omelet
set out on the table for her. She sat down and

partook of this simple meal, while the plain but
hearty people stood in the room and gazed at
her with joy and reverence.

From Kaslin Louisa proceeded to Danzig.
In Klemensfähr, at the crossing of the Nogat,
the merchants of Elbing had erected a canopy,
under which the royal pair were to take a rural

meal. The king had gone by way of Marien-
burg, that he might inspect the troops. In
consequence of this *detour* he was delayed. It
had already become late, and Louisa was asked
if she would have the meal served. She answered that she could not eat until her husband
arrived ; it was "the duty of a wife to wait for
her husband."

At Elbing a countryman, kneeling to the
king, presented to him a petition. Although
it had been forbidden to present petitions or
addresses on this journey, the king did not
strictly keep his command, but received several
of them, especially from the country people.
When this peasant, with his petition, prostrated himself before the king, the latter took
it, but said :

"A man should kneel before no man."

Their reception in Königsberg on the 3d of
June was one of unusual splendor. During
their stay there they occupied the magnificent
castle. Deputations waited on them to present

the united good wishes of the citizens, and the replies which the queen made to deputations went from mouth to mouth, and took root in all hearts. Daily large crowds assembled before the castle, that they might impress their royal guests with the love that filled their hearts. Louisa often appeared at the castle windows and greeted the multitude.

On the journey to Domnau, whither the king did not accompany the queen, Louisa was providentially saved from an accident. Through the carelessness of the coachman, the royal carriage was precipitated into a deep ravine and overturned. When the lady-in-waiting commenced scolding the frightened coachman for his want of foresight, Louisa quieted her by saying:

"Never mind; thank God that it is not worse; the people are more terrified than we are hurt."

On the 13th of June the king and queen entered Warsaw, the capital of the newly-acquired province of Poland, the siege of which Frederic William, as crown prince, had conducted a few years before. On the present occasion he had no military escort, and refused one, with the following reply:

" I am accustomed when traveling in my old provinces to be escorted only by the love of my people, and I am far from believing that I shall need any other escort in my new provinces."

An American authoress, Mrs. Julia M. Olin, has beautifully described their journey through Silesia in the following language:

" Cottages were gay with May blossoms, and roads strewn with rushes; citizens, with waving banners, lined the streets, and triumphal arches gave them welcome to Silesia. Groups of husbandmen sang Polish songs, burghers' daughters scattered roses before the royal guests; while the thunder of cannon, the ringing of bells, the flourish of trumpets and drums, gave loud expression to the general joy, which, at night, spoke to the eye in gardens, shops,

and docks brilliantly illuminated. Strains of
national music floated from wind instruments,
or were warbled by peasant girls ; rustic tem-
ples were erected in honor of the beautiful
queen, whose path was literally one of roses,
with such profusion were they strewn on the
way by the company of gardeners, male and
female, in their peculiar costume, gracefully
adorned with flowers.

"The scene at the bridge of the Oder was
one long to be remembered : the dark stream ;
the green island ; the ramparts ; the Jesuits'
College and Observatory ; the Elizabeth's Tower ; the living mass of people ; the balconies on
the bridge, in which stood fifty burghers'
daughters attired in white ; the German music
wafted from the tower above, and the Turkish
from the street below ; the students ranged in
double file welcoming their queen with a national air—all this composed a picture of rare
beauty." *

* " The Perfect Light," pp. 94-96.

In the month of August, 1800, the queen accompanied the king on another journey to this province, where he went to review his troops. The journey through this wild romantic country afforded her the purest pleasure. Some of these pictures must have ever remained vividly painted on her memory. The ascent of the Schneekoppe, the highest mountain in Germany, with its revelations of grandeur and beauty, awakened in Louisa the deepest emotions—"too much," she said, "for the heart to bear at once." The king uncovered his head in profound reverence, while the queen, with hands folded in prayer, stood silently by his side, feeling that this moment was one of the most blessed and solemn of her life, that she was elevated above this earth, and nearer to her God. We are reminded of Petrarch's meditations on the summit of Mount Venoux.

"If," thought he, "I have undergone so much labor in climbing this mountain that my body might be nearer to heaven, what ought I to do that my soul may be received into immortal regions ?"

The queen's pause of devotion was interrupted by shouts of loyalty from the crowd on the mountain side, and the thunder of the cannon on the adjacent heights, awakening prolonged echoes as they died away.

Not less impressive were the subterranean views which met the eye of the queen, three days afterward, in the mining works at Waldenburg. A boat conveyed them into the dark cavern out of which the stream issues, and which now glowed with an unwonted illumination. At the distance of every ten fathoms wax lights threw their radiance across the waters, and from a boat stationed seventy fathoms from the mouth of the cavern, mountain music gave to this weird and unearthly scene a still more impressive character. It was a picture for an artist—the wild groups of miners, the strongly-contrasted light and shadows, the beautiful

8

queen, in the dress and hat of a miner, that had been prepared for her, formed a picture to the dullest imagination.

It was never forgotten by those miners, and must have thrown a ray of light into their darkness, a proof of which was given in simple, earnest phrase by one of them, when, after a lapse of twenty-one years, Prince Radzivill, who made a similar excursion, asked if any of the miners present witnessed the royal visit on the 19th of August, 1800.

An honest old miner replied, in his straightforward homely dialect:

"Yes, above half of us are alive who had that honor; three of us are with you now. I sat at the rudder, and I could see the queen's sweet face well by the light of the lamps. In all my life I never saw such a face. She looked grand, as a queen should look; but she was gentle as a child, and had the sweetest smile I ever saw, just for all the world like my dead, blessed mother. As the psalm began,

'Praise the Lord, the mighty King of all the earth,' the queen took the king's hand and said softly, 'My favorite psalm ; this is heavenly ;' and then turning to me, said, 'More slowly, my good steersman.' The king and queen made us all presents, but she gave me with her own hand a little paper with two new Holland ducats, and I gave them to my wife, and she wears them for a necklace when she goes to church, or to take the sacrament, for what *that* queen had touched was holy. She was a woman indeed. Why did the good God take her away from us so soon ? She did every thing kindly, and loved us all. She told us that she took her mining dress with her to remind her of us."

The tears that rolled down his wrinkled cheeks, and stood in the eyes of the others who remembered the queen's visit, testified to the depth of the feeling she had awakened in their hearts.

A strikingly contrasted scene awaited her the same day. A picturesque and knightly

residence had been built by the Count von
Hockberg on the site of the ruins Vorstinberg,
formerly a fortress of the Middle Ages. The
new building on its rocky, wooded heights was
strictly in harmony with the feudal age, with
its tilting yard, moat, draw-bridge and portcul-
lis. On the watch-tower of the castle waved
the banner of Hockberg, guarded by a mailed
warrior. The trumpeters on the watch-tower
announced the arrival of strangers. An alarm
was sounded, the draw-bridge lowered, and the
heralds rode out of the gate to inquire the style
and title of the guests, who had ascended a bal-
cony opposite the castle gate. On its being
announced that it was their majesties of Prussia, the standard-bearer, accompanied by the
knights, requested permission to express their
sense of the honor done them by this royal
visit by a tournament. The troops of knights,
preceded by the standard-bearers, filed in solemn order, and when the banners were planted
the tilting matches began, and the victors re-

ceived their rewards—two medals of gold, and two of silver—from the hands of the queen, than whom a fairer never awarded the meed of knightly prowess.

Through an avenue of knights, with uplifted lances, the king and queen crossed the bridge and entered the castle, which in the evening was brilliantly illuminated. The window through which the queen looked upon the enchanting prospect below is still called " Louisa's view."

From this place Louisa journeyed homeward to Berlin, and on the 29th of June arrived at Charlottenburg. After the formal reception the king joined her.

In the following year they visited the western provinces of Westphalia and the present independent dukedoms of Anspach and Bayreuth, which at that time still belonged to Prussia. On this journey Louisa was permitted to see her nearest relatives at Frankfort-on-the-Main, Darmstadt, Hildburghausen, and the beautiful countries bordering on the Rhine and the Main, where she had passed her childhood.

But amid all this joyfulness, festivity, and beauty, there was much to fill a thoughtful Christian heart with sorrow. Unbelief, the result of the French false enlightenment, had nearly every-where taken root. While some were satisfied with a dry, unfruitful immorality, others had fallen back into an idolatry as gross as that of their ancestry.

When in Königsberg, and out enjoying a pleasure sail, the queen was handed by the throng a myrtle crown, on which was a poem, which read as follows:

> "With a gay surrounding
>   O'er the gleaming tide!   ·
> Comes a shallop bounding
>   With a god's fair bride!
>
> "Ah! it cometh toward me;
>   See what ne'er I saw!
> Imploringly I bend the knee:
>   Venus Amathusia!"

Venus, it will be remembered, was the goddess of love in the pantheons of Greece and Rome; and the epithet "Amathusia" was applied to her from Amathus, a city of very great antiquity, situated on the southern side of the Island of Cyprus, and dedicated to the worship of Venus.

At Wartenberg, in Posen, the burgesses had a temple erected, and decked with firs and wreaths of flowers. In the midst of it there was an altar with a flame rising from it, and around this eight young women, dressed in white, attended as high priestesses. By the side of the temple stood the Catholic and Protestant clergy. When the carriage of the queen arrived she was received with music, and six of the priestesses stepped out of the temple toward the carriage, while the two who remained behind strewed incense on the flame. In Breslau, Brandenburg-on-the-Havel, and Menel, where the Emperor Alexander of Russia and Frederic William III. met, there were inscriptions which read: "The allied gods." It is pleasing to know that Frederic William and Louisa were deeply grieved at this ridiculous idolatry.

A period so arrogant, and yet so false, could not but bring judgment upon itself. It was necessary that it be purified with fire. It makes one sad, however, to think that the queen must also, who was as a shining light in the darkness of the times, be purified in the crucible of affliction, that her faith and devotion might be still more strengthened.

IX.

Supremacy of Napoleon.

APOLEON I., Emperor of the French, had already commenced his victorious career. He had placed members of his own family on many of the thrones of Europe, and his ambition aimed at conquering the whole continent. He wrote in the year 1805 to his brothers in Naples and Holland "that Prussia and her allies should be crushed, and that this time he intended to finish up Europe." At this time Napoleon made deceiving offers of friendship to the King of Prussia, for he feared, with all his boldness, the Prussian power. When, in 1805, Russia, England, Austria, and Sweden invited the King of Prussia to join them in an alliance to overthrow the Emperor of the French, he would not, but remained neutral, wishing to hold out to his people the hope of peace. By this means Napoleon was enabled to evade the threatening danger, and Frederic William, in the meantime, prepared to defend his neutrality.

The passage of the French troops through Anspach, a part of Prussia which was neutral ground, was the first sign of the violation of the neutrality. Napoleon said it was essential for him to gain the necessary victory, and that he did not intend to lose it by any false hesitancy. And, indeed, he was by this act enabled to fall upon the Austrians and defeat them before they were prepared for him.

General Mack, the Austrian commander-in-chief, after losing several battles, was obliged to seclude himself in Ulm, and then surrender.

Such a breach of national law naturally roused the indignation of all who loved their country's honor. Queen Louisa was not a politician, but she was thoroughly German, and every insult offered to her country was branded upon her heart. About this time the tenth anniversary of her eldest son's birthday was celebrated at quiet Paretz. The young crown prince received from his father a present of a military hat and sword. When he appeared before his mother, for the first time, in the new uniform, she said to him with the deepest emotion :

" I hope, my son, when you use this dress, your first thought will be to avenge the wrongs of your unhappy countrymen."

Ten days after this the Emperor of Russia came to Berlin, and he and the King and Queen of Prussia went together to Potsdam. Alexander warned Frederic William of the danger that he was exposing himself to in remaining neutral.

"Prussia," he said, " cannot separate herself from the fate of Germany, from the affairs of Europe ; she does not make less certain, by her inactivity, the coming victory ; for a moment she would be spared, in order the more easily to be annihilated, when Austria and Russia had been settled ; but she would not the less surely become a prey to Napoleon's ambition."

Before leaving Berlin the Russian emperor expressed a desire to visit the tomb of Frederic the Great. The king immediately gave orders to have the royal vault in the garrison church illuminated, for it is there that the remains of the great king rest, and by his side lie the bones of his father, Frederic William I. Alexander, accompanied by the royal family, at midnight, went to the garrison church, and down into the illuminated vault. Overcome with emotion, he bowed down and kissed the coffin of Frederic the Great, and then reaching his hand over it to Frederic William, he vowed eternal friendship to him and the royal house, and bound himself by an oath to fight for the freedom of Germany. The queen witnessed this scene, and consecrated it with her tears.

At Potsdam a treaty was made, by which

Prussia, in common with Austria and Russia, was to offer terms of peace to the emperor of the French, and if he did not accept them, war would be declared on the 15th of December. Haugewitz, the minister, whom Frederic William had charged with the task of communicating with Napoleon, allowed the latter to influence him to defer the interview until he had gained a great victory over the Austrians, and then, contrary to his instructions, concluded a treaty, offensive and defensive, with the emperor. This took place on the 15th of December, the day that war was to have been declared.

Nor was this the only blind and treasonable act committed by the Prussian embassadors or ministers during those unhappy days. The citizens of Berlin were at that time divided into two classes. The one, the war party, wished Prussia to make common cause with Austria, Germany, and Europe, and draw the sword against France. The other, the peace party, or, more properly, the French party, who

saw safety for Prussia only in a close alliance
with France. To the latter party, unfortunately, not only belonged well-meaning men, but
unprincipled ones, who were in secret connection with Napoleon, and kept him advised of
the secrets of the Prussian government.

Louisa, who was not blind to the danger of
Germany and the Prussian throne, was deeply
afflicted. She had suffered much in health
since the winter of 1805, and the sorrow consequent on losing her youngest son, aged sixteen months, enfeebled her still more. In
heaviness of heart she went with the king to
Potsdam to spend the spring-time. In June
her physicians advised her to try the baths at
Pyrmont. There she was greatly rejoiced to
meet her father and eldest brother. After remaining six weeks at Pyrmont her health
became much improved, and she regained her
wonted spirits. She returned to Charlottenburg, that she might celebrate the king's birthday in their own home.

What was her surprise to learn, on arriving
there, that war had been declared against Napoleon, and that the army was ready to march
immediately. Although Louisa scarcely knew
what war was before it was determined upon,
she was accused afterward by Napoleon of
being the cause of it, having influenced the
king. It was what she *was*, not what she *did*,
that made her name a watchword for the ene-
mies of Napoleon. It was impossible for him,
with his tyrannically cold nature, to comprehend
the deeper feelings of the heart ; still he discovered that Queen Louisa was a great power, a
host in herself, which he could not otherwise
understand than by assigning to her a special
political activity, and on this account he did
not fail to calumniate her.

Although she took a deep interest in the fate
of the fatherland, she was never known to take
part in expressions of hate toward Napoleon.
She was too noble for that, and Frederic
William was of the same mind, notwithstanding

Napoleon's treachery. On a subsequent occasion, when a court lady manifested great displeasure at an honorable mention of Napoleon's name, Louisa made the following reply to her remark :

"We cannot overcome this affliction by hate. Resignation alone can mitigate it. We should think of Him who prayed for those who persecuted him."

This was her feeling, too, before the war. She was a lover of peace, and could not withhold her tears when she heard of the desolations of war in foreign lands.

In the middle of September Louisa accompanied her husband to Nauenburg, in the vicinity of the army. Although apparently full of courage and hope she felt the whole weight of the conflict, and was without confidence in the generalship of the Duke of Brunswick. Notwithstanding she saw the danger which threatened her country, her husband, her children, and all she loved, she called upon all to scorn it, and share with them whatever misfortune might be the result. On the 13th of October the queen appeared at Weimar before the departing troops, and inspired them by her courage and presence.

The first battle had been fought on the 10th of October, and this battle was soon followed by the two fatal onsets of Jena and Auerstadt on the 14th of October. These heavy defeats of the Prussians almost destroyed the hope which had been entertained for the welfare of the fatherland. The cannons were already thundering on the field of Jena when the queen unwillingly, at the urgent request of General Rüchel, left the head-quarters in order to return to Berlin. She had scarcely reached the gate of the capital when the news of the unparalleled defeat of the Prussian army reached her, and that Napoleon's soldiers were advancing into the open country. She immediately fled from Berlin with her children, and directed her steps eastward to Stettin.

9

In these first days of flight and treachery,
when one misfortune after another followed in
quick succession, the queen, in her woe, addressed these memorable words to her son, the
eldest prince, which express the deepest mater-
nal and national grief:

"You see me in tears; I weep for the decline
of my family, and the loss of that glory with
which our ancestors and their generals have
crowned the house of Hohenzollern, and whose
brightness has spread a luster over all who
obeyed that scepter. Oh, how dimmed is now
that brightness! Fortune destroys in a day an
edifice which for two hundred years great men
have been engaged in building. There is no
Prussian state, no Prussian army, and no Prussian national glory any more; it is vanished,
like the cloud which hid from us the horror
and danger of the fields of Jena and Auerstadt!
Ah, my son, you are of an age to understand
the great events by which we are now visited!
In the future, when your father and mother are

no more, call to mind this unhappy hour ; weep tears to my remembrance, as I weep now, at this fearful time, for the downfall of our father- land. But do not be satisfied with tears alone —act! Develop your powers! Perhaps the spirit of the guardian angel of Prussia will descend upon you. Deliver your country from the shame, reproach, and humiliation under which it groans. Try to regain the now tar- nished glory of our forefathers, as your great- grandfather, the Great Elector, once at Fehr- bellin revenged on the Swedes the defeat and disgrace of his father. Do not become a prey, my son, to the degeneracy of these times, but be a *man*, and aspire to the glory of becoming a great general and a hero! If you have this ambition you will be worthy of being called a prince and grandson of the great Frederic. If, however, you fail to lift up this fallen mon- archy, seek death as Louis Ferdinand sought it!"

The king and queen met at Küstrin, and

endured together the heart-rending news of the
surrender of fortifications and troops, as they
came in quick succession. While in Ortelsburg, on the 5th of December, 1806, the queen
wrote the following lines of the poet Goethe in
her diary, which we give in English :

> " Who never ate in tears his bread,
>   Who never, through the livelong night,
> Sat weeping on his anxious bed,
>   Knows not the great, the heavenly Might." *

We give here an incident, which we heard
related by a German lady, who is perfectly
familiar with the life and history of the queen.

When driven by the French from the palace
in Berlin the queen sought refuge one night
with her suite in a humble peasant's hut, and
while there, wrote with the diamond ring that

---

* " Wer nie sein Brod mit Thränen asz,
>   Wer nicht die kummervollen Nächte
> Auf seinem Bette weinend sass,
>   Der kennt euch nicht, ihr himmlischen Mächte."
—*Goethe's Sammtliche Werke.* Cotta's ed. Stuttgart,
1869. Vol. I, p. 249.

she wore upon her finger upon a pane of glass in the window this same verse of the poet Goethe, which, in her deep sorrows, had become to her a great favorite. The cottage is said to be still standing, and the lines perfectly visible on the glass.

She did not long continue in this state of grief, but dried her tears, and went to the piano and played and sang one of Paul Gerhardt's impressive hymns, which has been so beautifully rendered into English by John Wesley :—

> Commit thou all thy griefs
>   And ways into His hands,—
> To his sure trust and tender care
>   Who earth and heaven commands ;
> Who points the clouds their course,
>   Whom winds and seas obey :
> He shall direct thy wandering feet,—
>   He shall prepare thy way.
>
> Thou on the Lord rely,
>   So, safe, shalt thou go on ;
> Fix on his work thy steadfast eye,
>   So shall thy work be done.

No profit canst thou gain
By self-consuming care ;
To him commend thy cause—his ear
Attends the softest prayer.

In the midst of her greatest anguish she did not fully lose her courage and confidence. While others, who had at first been so sanguine of success, and who had now lost all sense of honor, and even fidelity, and advised submission to the conqueror, she advised firm resistance. " Only determined resistance can save us," she said. But there were moments when the question would rise, whether the withstanding of Napoleon were not a defiance of fate.

X.

Sunshine and Shadows.

FROM Ortelsburg the royal family proceeded toward Wehlau, and thence to Königsberg. Every post brought them news of fresh disasters. The strongest fortifications were given up almost without any resistance. The news of these overwhelming defeats so affected the queen's health that she was prostrated with a low, nervous fever, and for fourteen days her life was in the greatest danger. Before she had fully recovered her strength, they were obliged to continue their flight to Memel. When the remnant of the Prussian army joined the Russians the fighting began again, and the queen returned to Königsberg. Here she kept up a correspondence with the most superior men, with the court minister, Barowsky, and the Councilor of War, Schneffner. They animated her patriotism, and confirmed her Christian faith. She needed support, for every thing seemed lost. They were obliged again to flee to Memel.

In May, 1807, at the commencement of the new campaign, she was full of hope, and wrote the following to her father :—

"Yes, best of fathers, I am convinced that all will yet go well, and we shall all be happy again. The siege of Danzig goes on finely ; the people behave nobly ; they assist in making easy the duties of the soldiers ; they give them food and wine, and will not listen to surrender. They would rather be burned under the ruins of their houses than be unfaithful to the king. The same is true with reference to Colberg and Graudenz. Would that it had been so with all the strongholds ! But enough of past evils. We will turn our eyes to God, to him who orders our fate, and who will not forsake us if we will not forsake him.

"The king, with the Emperor Alexander, is with the army, and he will remain there as long as the latter does. This unity, proved by constancy in misfortune, gives ground for the greatest hope. I am convinced that through steadfastness, and that only, we shall conquer sooner or later."

This last hope vanished with the defeat of the allied armies at Friedland, on the 14th of June. Königsberg was taken by the French, and the queen, who was now in Memel, prepared to leave the kingdom. At this time she wrote again to her father, and we extract from her letters the principal passages.

"Do not think, dear father, that I have given way to pusillanimity. There are two things which sustain me : the first is the thought that we are not the toys of fortune, but are in the hands of God, and that his providence guides us ; the other is, that we fall honorably. Prussia will not bear the chains of a slave willingly. The king could not have done otherwise than

he has done without being untrue to, and a be-
trayer of, his people.   If I leave the kingdom it
will only be through the urgency of necessity.
I turn my eyes, however, to Heaven, whence all
good must invariably come, and my firm faith
is that we will not have more to endure than
we can bear.   All things come from Thee,
thou Merciful Father!   My *faith* does not
waver, although I can *hope* no more.   To live
and die truly, and if necessary live upon bread
and salt, cannot make me unhappy, but I have
lost all hope.   If prosperity should come, no
one will be happier than I; but I do not anticipate it.   If further misfortune come, it may
amaze me for a moment, but it never can cast
me down entirely, so long as it is not deserved.
But any wrong on our side would bring me to
the grave; I could not survive it, for we are
placed in a high position."

A letter to Madame de Krudener, for whom
she had the greatest admiration, and who had
joined her in the days of her deepest grief at

Königsberg, testifies to the depth of the queen's religious life :

" I owe a confession to your excellent heart," she writes, "and I am convinced that you will receive it with tears of joy. You have made me better than I was before. Your words of truth, our conversations on religion and Christianity, have made the deepest impression upon my mind. I have entered with deeper earnestness into the things, the existence and value of which I had indeed felt before, but had rather imagined than positively known. These contemplations had very comforting results for me. I came nearer to God ; my faith became stronger, and thus, in the midst of misfortune, and many injuries and griefs, I have never been without comfort, never quite unhappy. Add to this the goodness of the God of love, who never hardened my heart, but always kept it open to the kindliness and love of my fellow-creatures. That goodness always filled me with an impulse to help and be useful to them.

"You will understand that I can never be quite miserable while I have this source of purest joy. With the keen eye of truth I have seen the vanity of earthly greatness, and its nothingness in comparison with heavenly possessions. Yes, I have attained to a repose of the soul, and an inward peace, which allow me to hope that I may be able to bear all God's dispensations, and the sorrows that are sent to purify me, with the composure and humility of a true Christian. For it is in this light that I view all the severe trials which bow us down. I have found myself again in the tumult of the world. Promise that you will still always tell me the whole truth."

The queen wrote again in September, 1808:

"Have you heard that the king has commanded that memorial tablets shall be placed in the churches for those who have fought for their Fatherland, to the memory of the dead, to the honor of the survivors, and for the emulation of others? This is another spark from which may be kindled the flame from God which shall consume the scourge of nations. Has it not been lighted in the Tyrol as well as in Spain?

" ' Freedom upon the mountains.'

Do not these words, which I now, for the first time, understand, sound like a prophecy when you look at those mountains, and see what a rising there has been at the call of Höfer! What a man this Andreas Höfer is! A peasant becomes a general, and what a general he makes! Prayer is his weapon, and God his ally.

" He fights with folded hands, he fights on bended knee, and smites with the cherubim's flaming sword. And these faithful Swiss, who were before familiar to my mind through Pestalozzi, childlike in spirit—they fight like the Titans, rolling masses of rock from the mountains. The same is true in Spain. If the times of the Maid of Orleans should come again, and if the enemy should be overcome at last, it might be by that power by which the French, with a maiden at their head, drove the foe from their land. Ah, how many times I have read it over and over again ! "

The court-minister, Barowsky, gives us an insight into the deep workings of the Holy Spirit on her mind. He says :

" With the feeling and expression of timidity she approaches the holy truths of religion, but also with an expression of thirst and longing, and she receives refreshment from them in all their purity. What pleases me the most is that all her views, convictions, and endeavors are firmly founded on the revealed word of God ; this gives her firmness, assurance, coherence, and repose ; and since she honors me with her confidence, I endeavor to confirm her faith. In her prevailing state of mind she sympathizes most particularly with the Psalms ; the holy enthusiasm which pervades them is in harmony with her beautiful and poetic nature,

and gives an impulse to her pious spirit. The
grave experiences of her life open to her the
inmost meanings of the Holy Scriptures, and
guide her into their full and deep meaning.
The true old proverb, 'Trouble teaches us to
mark and understand the Word,' is gloriously
illustrated in her, and I am often most agreeably surprised by her spiritual and intellectual
remarks, questions, and answers.

"When I had the honor to wait on her last
Sunday I found her alone in her sitting-room
reading the Bible. She rose quickly, and met
me in the most friendly manner, at once beginning: 'Now I have thought over and felt the
preciousness of the 126th psalm, about which
we were talking. The more I meditate on it,
and try to grasp its meaning, the more its loveliness and sublimity attract me; and I do not
know any thing which has such a solemn, be-
nign, elevating, and comforting effect upon my
mind as these precious words. The anguish of
soul which is simply expressed in them is deep,

but tranquil, peaceful, and tender. What it will effect, and the fruit which it will bring forth, are strikingly explained under the pleasing figure of seed-time and harvest. The hope which soars above all, and makes all sorrow endurable, is like the hues of morning, and you hear in the distance the triumphal songs of the victor rising above the tumult of the waves of sorrow. It is pervaded by a spirit of melancholy, but also of victory, of resignation, and the most joyful trust; it is an elegy, but also a hymn of praise — a halleluia mingled with tears. I look at this psalm as you look at a lovely flower on which a dewdrop glistens in the morning light. I have read it again and again, until it is firmly impressed upon my memory.'

"And then with an expression of holy reverence, with a low, but firm and clear voice, and in a tone of the purest devotion, the queen repeated the psalm which was engraven on her mind, occasionally altering it to adapt it to her own circumstances. As a beautiful hymn sweetly sung makes a deeper and more lively impression than when read, the well-known words, as I heard them from the queen, gave rise to new feelings. For her melodious manner of reciting it, though it was not exactly intoned, was like an ecstatic song, poured forth from her pure heart. As I listened to and looked at this exalted and enlightened woman, with the words of everlasting life on her eloquent lips, the words came into my mind, 'In thy light shall we see light,' and, 'Blessed are they that mourn, for they shall be comforted.' Every thing became clearer to me than before, and she appeared more beautiful than ever."

10

XI.

At Tilsit.

EGOTIATIONS for peace were opened in Tilsit, and the king's advisers believed that the presence of the queen at head-quarters would greatly facilitate the negotiations, and secure better terms. Napoleon himself had a great desire to see her. She, therefore, returned from Memel to Tilsit.

"What resignation it cost me," she wrote in her diary, "God only knows; for, though I do not hate the man, I look upon him as the author of the unhappiness of the king and his people. I admire his talents; but his character, so cunning and false, I cannot like. It will be difficult for me to be polite and gracious to him; still the effort is demanded, and I must make the sacrifice."

Interview with Napoleon.

On the evening of the 4th of July Louisa reached Puktupöhnen, a village near Tilsit, where the king was stopping. Napoleon immediately sent to inquire if Her Majesty would show him the honor of dining with him, and that he would, with her permission, call and see her on her arrival in town. She answered affirmatively, and an hour after her arrival in Tilsit the emperor approached with a large escort.

It was not a light task which devolved upon the indisposed queen, to receive such a visitor. She understood well, however, how to treat him with politeness, tact, and self-possession.

When he had ascended the stairs she greeted him in a friendly manner, but with dignity. After a few words on ordinary topics, Louisa spoke of the reasons that had brought her to Tilsit:

"I came to ask you, Emperor, to grant a favorable peace to Prussia."

In reply to this, Napoleon asked, in a some-what contemptuous tone,

" How could you commence war with me ? "

" Sire," answered the queen, " it was the glory of Frederic the Great which led us to be deceived in our strength, if we have deceived ourselves."

This conversation, in which Napoleon brought up every thing, in order, by his en-tangling questions, to embarrass the queen, lasted three quarters of an hour. How much Louisa suffered then, more for the sake of others than herself, she remembered afterward with tears.

" I was only a woman, a weak woman," she wrote, " and yet I rose high above the ad-versaries, who were so poor and timid of heart."

At the sumptuous banquet which the em-peror had prepared for his guests, the place of honor assigned to the queen was on the right hand of Napoleon, while the king sat on his left.

"The strength of character and spirit of this princess or queen," so wrote a renowned French writer and admirer of Napoleon, "made itself felt in the conversation, so that the emperor himself was embarrassed, who, though nothing wanting in politeness to her, let not a word escape which would in any way commit him. During the repast she endeavored to draw from him some word of hope in behalf of Magdeburg."

The king deported himself in a silent and dignified manner. Napoleon tried to comfort him for the sacrifice of his hereditary kingdom, by saying it was the common vicissitude of war. Whereupon the king answered, in the anguish of his heart, that he, Napoleon, might speak lightly of it, for he knew not what it was to lose an hereditary kingdom, with which the dearest associations of youth were bound, as to one's cradle.

"What cradle!" exclaimed Napoleon, laughing. "When a child grows up it has no more time to think about its cradle."

"Still," answered the king to the emperor, "a man can no more forget his youth than he can disown it, and a man of feeling will gratefully remember the cradle in which he lay as a child."

Such home thrusts as these were not calculated to win one who had always been used to flattery. But it was impossible for the king to dissemble.

Napoleon, on his departure, offered the queen a very rare and beautiful rose. At first she seemed inclined to refuse it, but finally took it, saying:

"At least with Magdeburg."

But the emperor answered uncourteously:

"Remember, your majesty, that it is in my power to *offer*, and only in your majesty's to *accept*."

A dignified silence was most appropriate to

such a response. He knew too well, on this
sad day to Prussia, how to embarrass and hu-
miliate the queen. But her noble and self-pos-
sessed appearance made a deep impression on
his mind, and he had previously determined, on
her account, on giving easy terms of peace; but
he recalled to mind the warning of his great
minister, Talleyrand, who had said to him,

"Sire, shall posterity say that you have not
profited by your great conquests because of a
beautiful woman?"

On the 9th of July, therefore, the treaty of
peace was signed at Tilsit, which was so crush-
ing for Prussia, and on the 10th the king and
queen departed for Memel.

"The peace is concluded," she wrote, this
day, "but at a fearful price! Our boundaries
in the future only extend to the Elbe; yet the
king is greater than his adversary. After the
battle of Eylau he could have made an advan-
tageous peace; but then he would have been
obliged to negotiate with Napoleon, and go

against Russia; while now he has been compelled to negotiate through necessity, and will not enter into an alliance with him. That will bring blessing hereafter to Prussia; that, at least, is my firm belief."

XII.

Letter to Her Father.

THE following letter of the queen, the
most remarkable and interesting of
all, shows how thorough an understanding she had of the position of her country; it also gives us a glimpse of her domestic
and matrimonial happiness, and of the talents
and dispositions of her children.

She wrote in the spring of 1808:

"BEST OF FATHERS:—It is all over with us,
if not forever, at least for the present. I hope
for nothing more during this life. I have resigned myself, and in this resignation, this
submission to the will of Heaven, I am at rest
and in great peace, and if not happy in an
earthly sense, I am, of what is more importance,

mentally happy. I see with increasing clearness that it was necessary for every thing to happen as it has happened. Divine Providence is imperceptibly introducing a new order of things into the world, while the old order is passing away. We have been slumbering on the laurels of Frederic the Great, who, the foremost man of his century, created a new era. We have not advanced with this age, and therefore it has passed on and left us behind. To no one is this clearer than to the king. I have had a long conversation with him on the subject, and he said penitently, 'We must do differently.'

" The best and most considerate are sometimes misled, and the French emperor, at least, is more wary and cunning. If the Russians and the Prussians had fought as bravely as lions, we would have been compelled to leave the enemy with the advantage, if not actually the victor. From Napoleon we can learn much, and the lesson will not be forgotten. It were blasphemy to say, 'God be with him;' still, he is visibly an instrument in the hands of the Almighty to put an end to the old order of things, and inaugurate a new age. Faith in a perfect Being assures us that better times will certainly come. But it can only work good for the world *through the good;* and for this reason I do not believe that the Emperor Napoleon Bonaparte is so very secure upon his, at present, brilliant throne. Truth and righteousness alone can give peace and security, while he is only politically wise, acting according to circumstances, and not according to the laws of eternity. He has blotted his reign with many sins. He does not endeavor to elevate good men and good things, but thinks only of his own immeasurable ambition and his own interest. One is more amazed than pleased with what he does. He is blinded by his success, and imagines he can accomplish every thing. He is entirely without moderation, and without that a man soon loses his equilibrium and falls.

I believe firmly in God, and I also believe in a
moral supervision of the world.

"But this supervision I cannot reconcile
with the dominion of mere power, and therefore I hope that the present evil time will be
followed by a better. It is hoped for and expected by the better class of men, and we must
not be led astray by the praise lavished upon
the great hero of the day. It is evident to all
that what has happened, and is happening, is
not for the ultimate good, but the opening of
the way to a better future. That future, however, appears far distant, and we shall not
probably ever live to see it. As God wills ; all
things as he wills. In this hope I find comfort, strength, courage, and cheerfulness. Is
not every thing in this world transitory ? Yet
we must pass through it ; and it should be our
greatest care, as it is our greatest duty, to become each day riper and better.

"Here, dear father, you have my political
confession of faith, as well as I, a woman, can

fashion it and set it forth. It may have its
faults, and you must, therefore, excuse my
troubling you with it. But you see, at least,
by it, that you have a daughter who is pious
and resigned under reverses, and that the foun-
dation of Christian faith, which she owes to
your instruction and example, has had its fruit,
and will have so long as life lasts.

"You will be pleased to hear, dear father,
that the misfortune which has fallen upon us
has not affected our domestic happiness ; indeed, it seems to have drawn us nearer together, and strengthened our affections. The
king, who is the best of men, is kinder than
ever. Often I fancy that I see in him the
lover and the bridegroom ; more in actions
than in words do I perceive his constant devotion to me. Only yesterday he said to me,
looking at me with his guileless eyes and earnest expression of countenance, 'Dear Louisa,
thou hast become dearer and more precious
than ever to me in misfortune. Now I know

by experience what I possess in thee. Let the storm continue without, as it will; if only our happiness remain undisturbed, we are secure. Because I love thee so fondly, I have desired our youngest-born little daughter to be called Louisa. May she become a Louisa!' This tenderness on his part affected me to tears. It is my pride, my joy, and my happiness to possess the love of the best of men, and because I love him in return with all my heart, and we are so united that the will of the one is the will of the other, it is very easy for us to preserve this harmony day by day. Indeed, he pleases me in all things, and I please him in all things, and we are never so happy as when together. Pardon me, dear father, if I say this in a certain vain-glorious manner; it is the artless expression of my joy, in which no one in the world takes a deeper interest than you, my good father. I have also learned from the king to do good to others, of which I must not write; it is enough that *we* know it.

"Our children are our real treasures, and in them we place our fondest hopes.

"The crown prince is full of life and spirit. He has splendid talents, which have already begun to develop. He is truthful in all his perceptions and expressions. He is very zealous in the study of history, and is deeply impressed by the great and the good. He has much inclination to humor, and his comical, overdrawn ideas afford us much entertainment. He is particularly attached to his mother, and could not be purer minded than he is. I love him most tenderly, and often speak to him of the duties which will devolve upon him if he lives to become king.

"Our son William will, if I am not mistaken, take after his father, and be plain, honest, and of good understanding. He resembles him also in personal appearance, only, I think, that he will not be so handsome. You see, dear father, that I am still deeply enamored with my husband.

"Our daughter Charlotte every day gives me more joy. She is reserved, and lives much within herself. But within an apparently cold exterior she possesses a warm, generous heart, showing that there is something gentle in her nature. If she only embraces Christianity, I anticipate for her a brilliant future. Carl is good-natured, joyful, honest, and talented. He is developing physically as well as mentally, and his *naïvete* often makes us laugh. His never-ending questions not unfrequently throw me into embarrassment, because I cannot answer them. They exhibit a great thirst for knowledge. I am convinced that he will go through life joyously, but not without being sensible of the joys and sorrows of others. Alexandrine is, as is natural with children of her age and disposition, childish and insinuating. She exhibits good understanding and a lively imagination. She has a fondness for the ridiculous, and shows much talent for satire, but without marring her good-nature. Of little Louisa, much cannot yet be said. She has the profile and eyes of her father. I wish that she may become like her amiable and pious grandmother, Louisa of Orange, wife of the great elector.

" Now, dear father, I have conducted you through my whole gallery. You will say that it is like any partial mother, who sees all the goodness and beauty in her children, but is blind to all their failings and faults. I cannot find any thing in them to give me cause for anxiety in the future. Our children, like all other children, have their whims and peculiarities ; but, as they grow older, they will learn how to correct them.

" Circumstances educate men, and I trust that our children will be benefited by seeing, while so young, the earnest and serious side of life. Had they been thrown into the lap of luxury and ease, they might have thought that it would always be so ; but that it *can be otherwise* they now see by the serious countenance

11

of their father and the frequent tears of their
mother. It will prove especially beneficial to
the crown prince in the future, that he has
become . acquainted with misfortune in his
youth. It will teach him how to value prosperity when it comes, as I hope it will, and
how to make beneficent use of it. My
thoughts are wholly centered in my children,
and it is my daily prayer that God will bless
them, and give them his Holy Spirit. If God
preserve our good children he will preserve our
best treasures, which no one can tear from us.
Then, let what will occur, in the society of our
dear children we shall be happy.

" I write this to you, my beloved father, that
you may think of us in tranquillity. I commend my husband to your fatherly remembrance, and my children also, who, with this
letter, kiss the hands of their venerable grandfather. I remain, dear father,

"Your sincere daughter,

" Louisa."

XIII.

The Romance of a Ring.

AS the betrothal and marriage of the daughter Charlotte to the Grand Duke Nicholas, afterward Emperor of Russia, whose character Louisa partially describes in this letter to her father, forms one of the sweetest and most romantic love-episodes in the history of European courts, we give it, as taken from a recent work :—

Charlotte was just sixteen when, in the year 1814, the Grand Duke Nicholas, on his way to the camp of the allied armies in France, passed through Berlin, and was warmly welcomed as an honored guest at the royal palace.

The description which those who saw and knew the grand duke at that time have given of the incomparable graces of his person and mind makes it easy for us to imagine that the heart of a young girl just budding into womanhood was captivated and charmed by him almost at first sight. Well he might have said, like Cæsar, "I came, I saw, I conquered." The princess fell in love with him, and, fortunately for her, the young grand duke returned her love fully as passionately.

The Grand Duke Nicholas had the reputation of being one of the handsomest, if not the very handsomest, man of his times; and his majestic and stately form, which measured no less than six feet and two inches, was considered unequaled in beauty, not only in Russia, but in all Europe. He was vigorous, strong, full of life and health, with broad shoulders and chest, while his small hands and feet were of the most aristocratic elegance; his whole figure realized the perfect model of manly and commanding beauty which the divine art of a sculptor of antiquity has immortalized under the features of the Apollo Belvidere. His

features were of the Grecian cast—forehead
and nose formed a straight line—and his large
blue, sincere eyes showed a singular combina-
tion of composure, sternness, self-reliance, and
pride, among which it would have been difficult
for the observer to name the predominant expression. Those who would have looked closely and attentively into those remarkable eyes
would have easily believed that their threatening glances would suffice to suppress a rebel-
lion, to terrify and disarm a murderer, or to
frighten away a supplicant ; but there would
have been but few to believe that the sternness
of these eyes could be so entirely softened as to
beam forth nothing but love and kindness.
Among these few was, however, the young
Prussian princess, who had drunk deep in their
intoxicating fervor. It is true that she was the
only person in the world in whose presence the
Olympian gravity of his features gave way to a
radiant cheerfulness, which made his manly
beauty perfectly irresistible.

In such moments his magnificent brow, always the seat of meditation and thought, exhibited the serene beauty and Attic grace of a young Athenian ; the serious Pericles seemed, by the invisible wand of a magician, to have been transformed into the youthful Alcibiades.

Such is the flattering picture which his contemporaries have drawn of the personal appearance of the Grand Duke Nicholas at the time of his arrival at Berlin.

At that time, however, the matchless personal charms of the grand duke were not enhanced by political prospects of the most exalted character. He was not even eventually considered an heir to the imperial crown of Russia. It is true, Alexander I., his brother, had no children, but in the case of his death, which could not be expected soon, the Grand Duke Constantine was to inherit the throne of Peter the Great, and leave to Nicholas at best but the position of a prince of the first blood.

Nevertheless, Frederick William, charmed alike by the beauty and intellect of his guest, and by the hope of uniting the sovereign houses of Prussia and Russia by the close ties of a family union, greeted the prospect of a marriage between the grand duke and his daughter with enthusiasm, especially when he discovered that the young folks themselves were very fond of each other.

The king then delicately insinuated to his daughter that if she had taken a liking to the grand duke, and had reason to believe that the prince entertained similar feelings toward her, their marriage would meet with no objection on his part.

But the young princess, although secretly delighting in a hope which so fully responded to the secret wishes of her heart, was either too proud or too bashful to confess to her father her love for the grand duke, who had not yet made any declaration to her.

In this manner the day approached on

which the grand duke was to leave Berlin. On the eve of his departure a grand gala supper was given in his honor at the royal palace, and, by way of accident or policy, the young Princess Charlotte was seated by the side of her distinguished admirer.

The grand duke was uncommonly taciturn during the evening. His high forehead was clouded, and his gloomy eyes seemed to follow in the space vague phantoms flitting before his imagination. Repeatedly he neglected to reply to questions addressed to him, and when he was asked to respond to a toast which one of the royal princes had proposed in his honor, he seemed to awake from a profound dream which had entirely withdrawn him from his surroundings.

Suddenly, as if by a mighty effort of his will, he turned to his fair neighbor, and whispered so as only to be understood by her :—

"So I shall leave Berlin to-morrow!"

He paused abruptly, and looked at the princess, as if he was waiting for an answer which expressed sorrow and grief on her part. But the princess was fully as proud as the grand duke, and, overcoming the violent throbbing of her heart, she said politely to him :—

"We are all very sorry to see your Imperial Highness leave us so soon. Would it not have been possible for you to defer your departure?"

"You will all be very sorry?" muttered the grand duke, not entirely satisfied with the vagueness of sorrow which these words of the princess implied. "But you in particular, madame?" he added, after some hesitation. "For it will depend on you alone whether I shall stay here or depart."

"Ah!" replied Charlotte, with her sweetest smile, "and what have I to do to keep your Imperial Highness here?"

"You must permit me to address my admiration and homage to you."

"Is that all?"

"And you must encourage me to please you."

"That is much more difficult," said the princess, with a deep blush, but at the same time her eyes beamed forth so much affection and delight that the prince could see at a glance that his fondest hopes had been realized beforehand.

"During my short stay at Berlin," the grand duke continued in the same tone of voice, "I have taken pains to study your character and your affections, and this study has satisfied me that you would render me very happy, while, on the other hand, I have some qualities which I think would secure your happiness."

The princess was overcome by emotion, and in her confusion did not know what to answer. At last she said, "But here, in the presence of the whole court, at the public table, you put such a question to me!"

"O," replied the prince, "you need not make any verbal reply. It will be sufficient for you to give me some pledge of your affection. I

see there on your hand a small ring whose possession would make me very happy. Give it to
me."

"What do you think of it, here in the presence of a hundred spectators?"

"Ah, it can be easily done without being
seen by any body. Now we are chatting so
quietly with each other that there is not one
among the guests who suspects in the least
what we are speaking about. Press the ring
into a morsel of bread, and leave it on the
table; I will take the talisman, and nobody
will notice it."

"This ring is really a talisman."

"I expected so. May I hope to hear its
history?"

"Why not? My first governess was a Swiss
lady, by the name of Wildermatt. Once she
went to Switzerland in order to enter upon
an inheritance which had been bequeathed to
her by a distant relative. When she came
back to Berlin, a few weeks afterward, she

showed me quite a collection of pretty and costly jewelry, which formed part of the inheritance. 'This is a curious old ring,' said I to her as I put this little old-fashioned ring on my finger. 'Does it not look queer and cunning? Perhaps it is an old relic or talisman, and may have been worn centuries ago by a pious lady, who had received it from her knight, starting for the Holy Land.' I tried to take the ring from my finger again, but I could not get it off, for I was a little fleshier then than now," said Charlotte, smilingly. "My governess insisted on my keeping the ring as a souvenir. I accepted her present, and the ring has been on my finger ever since. Some time afterward, when I was contemplating its strange workmanship, I succeeded in pulling it from my finger, and was much surprised at seeing engraved on the inside some words which, though nearly rubbed out by the wear of time, were still legible. Now, your Imperial Highness, what do you think were the words engraved upon it? I think when you hear them you will take some interest in the ring."

"Ah! and pray what were they?"

"The words engraved upon the inside were, '*Empress of Russia.*' This ring had undoubtedly been presented by an Empress of Russia to a relative of Madame Wildermatt, for I was told that both this lady and her mother had formerly belonged to the household of the czarina, your august grandmother."

"This is really remarkable," said the grand duke, thoughtfully. "I am quite superstitious, and I am really inclined to regard this ring, if I should be happy enough to receive it from you as a pledge of your love, as an omen of very auspicious significance."

In answer to this second, and even more direct, appeal to her heart, the princess took a small piece of bread, played carelessly with it, and managed to press the ring into the soft crumbs. Then she dropped it playfully on the table quite close to the plate of her neighbor.

And after this adroit exhibition of her skill as an actress she continued to eat as unconcernedly as if she had performed the most insignificant action of her life.

With the same apparent coolness and indifference the grand duke picked up the bread inclosing the ring, took the latter out of its ingenious envelope, and concealed it in his breast, for it was too small to fit any of his fingers. It was this ring—both the pledge of Charlotte's love and the auspicious omen of his own elevation to the imperial dignity—which Nicholas wore on a golden chain around his neck to the very last day of his life, and which, if we are not mistaken, has even descended with him into the vault of his ancestors.

Three years after, in 1817, Princess Charlotte, then only nineteen years of age, and in the full splendor of beauty and happiness, made her entry into St. Petersburg by the side of her husband, whose eye had never looked prouder, and whose Olympian brow had never been more serene than at this happiest moment of his life. As he looked down upon the vast multitude who had gathered from every quarter of the vast empire to greet the young princess with shouts and rejoicings, and then again upon his fair young bride, perhaps the inscription of the ring recurred to his mind, for, bending his head quite close to the ear of Charlotte, he whispered, "Now empress of the hearts, and some day, perhaps, empress of the realm."

At this moment the procession reached the main entrance of the Winter Palace, where Alexander I., the emperor, surrounded by a brilliant suit of generals and courtiers, came to meet his beautiful sister-in-law, and conducted her into the sumptuous drawing-rooms of this magnificent palace of the czars. This palace was rebuilt in one year at a great sacrifice of human life. Six thousand men were required to be constantly employed, and many out of this number died daily on account of the extreme heat necessary for its completion—all of this to carry out the caprice of one man. It is considered one of the most extensive and magnificent royal structures in any country. Who would believe that eight short years afterward the brilliant young emperor had breathed his last, and that Nicholas and Charlotte would succeed him on the throne of Russia? The Grand Duke Constantine, the legitimate heir to the throne, having no desire to reign, and having no legal heir, resigned the crown in his favor. Truly the inscription of the engagement-ring had proven prophetic !*

* Monroe, "Public and Parlor Readings," pp. 205 ff.

XIV.

After the Years of Sorrow.

IN these troublous times Louisa occupied
herself much with the study of history,
wishing to live in the past, as the future
had lost all its attractiveness for her. Especially was she interested in the history of Germany in the olden times. The motto of the
good old days of the knights, "Justice, faith,
and love," pleased her so much, that she had it
engraved on a seal. At this time she said,
were she to choose a motto for herself it should
be, "God is my confidence."

She saw, too, in the re-awakening of Christianity, the dawn of morning after a long night,
and was once more filled with the hope that
the people of Prussia, and indeed of all Germany, humbled by the severe judgments of

God, would again rise to power, and be able to throw off the foreign yoke.

The queen was a zealous advocate of education, and exerted herself for its advancement, for she knew what a powerful influence it would have on the rising generation. She read with great pleasure and profit Pestalozzi's celebrated book, " Lienhard and Gertrude." The following passage especially pleased her : " Sorrow and misery, if they are endured, are blessings of God."

Pestalozzi was the closing member in one of the most remarkable educational groups that have arisen in history. His good predecessors were Herder, Basedow, Campe, and Salzmann ; but in the one department of thorough educational reform he was the greatest of them all. Some of his critics have alleged that his sympathies with Christianity were not strong ; but in practical life, and particularly in his labors for poor children, he exhibited the true Christian spirit. In 1775 he founded his " Poor

School for the Children of Beggars ;" but it was in 1798 that his true greatness shone forth the brightest, when he fed and clothed the children saved from the smoking ruins of Stanz, in Switzerland. He was the only father the orphans had. He slept with them, and would not leave them until the storm of war drove him away.

His idea was, in his entire educational system, to develop what was native to the child, and not merely to fill the mind with foreign material. IIe held, that by discipline in self-exercise the intellect receives its highest development. With the beginning of the present century his reputation became world-wide. His theory of education grew to be the common property of Europe, and still prevails in the schools of all civilized lands. We are not surprised that his efforts to relieve the poor and improve the minds of children should enlist the profound sympathy of Louisa. It was his noble heart that attracted her attention, and made her one of the best and truest friends of education, even amid her country's prostration.

The Emperor Alexander, at this time, gave King William and Queen Louisa a very urgent invitation to visit St. Petersburg, hoping that they might, by a little change and recreation, revive their drooping spirits. Accordingly on the 27th of December, 1808, they set out for the Russian capital, attended by a very small escort.

" It was in the deep winter-time, and costly robes of fur were presented to the royal guests and their suite. The post-houses were newly built, and furnished for their reception ; discharges of cannon thundered out their stentorian welcome—groups of peasants on horseback in their national costume awaited them— sledges, with princely appointments and escorts, bore them swiftly over the icy roads, and thirty thousand troops lined the streets of St. Petersburg as they drove to the palace—the queen herself riding in a carriage which, with delicate consideration to her feelings, was built after the model of the one she used when in Königsberg.

" Twelve elegant rooms were appropriated to the queen—one with hangings of pale pink silk, draped with delicate muslin, with a toilette of gold ; and a basket containing six superb Turkish shawls was presented to her.

" The night of her arrival St. Petersburg was brightly defined by lines of light, dazzling the eye with their brilliancy. Magnificent presents, contrasting strangely in their royal splendor with the frugal fare and simple rooms of Memel, awaited her acceptance on New Year's Day—crystal vases with glass pedestals six feet high—exquisite porcelain vases—a sumptuous table-service of crystal, India shawls, and other costly articles. On this day a brilliant wedding took place—the Duchess Catherine, the emperor's sister, being united to the Prince of Oldenburg."*

Each day brought a new feast, but Louisa

* "The Perfect Light," pp. 123-4.

felt more saddened than rejoiced by the splendor. More pleasure was afforded her by the benevolent institutions which she visited than by any thing else. She visited one of these, in company with the dowager empress, which supported three hundred and sixty young girls. She readily appreciated the great value of such establishments, and made minute observations, that she might be able to found others in her own country. Unfortunately she did not live to see the realization of this wish. There was one, however, consecrated to her memory on the first anniversary of her death, its aim being to develop in the women of the future the piety, purity of heart, beauty of soul, truth, and faith, which were so beautifully resplendent in the character of their departed queen. Louisa visited with equal interest the hospital for foundlings, founded by Catherine II.

In Riga, among other places of interest, the royal pair were shown the Guildhall of the "Black Heads," a society dating from the year

1390, the members of which took the vow
never to marry.

" If you had belonged to this society," said
the king to Louisa; "you would have been
spared your sad experience."

The queen answered:

" Had our trouble been ten times as great as
it has been, and you had told me of it previously, you would not have made me become
a member."

These uninterrupted festivities continued
until the 31st of January, 1809, when the king
and queen returned again to Königsberg. On
her return she wrote as follows:

" I have returned as I went. Nothing daz-
zles me any more. My kingdom is not of this
world."

Men like Von Stein and Gneisenau judged
the journey harshly. The latter wrote:

" The king has been in a bad humor since
his return. He scolds about trifles in the service. At St. Petersburg he saw the Russians

dressed up for reviews. Certainly the half-slaughtered East Prussians are a contrast to them. Every thing must look very insignificant to him after the pomp there; his half-monarchy, his half-palace, the half romance of the last few years; but this is all in harmony with half measures."

Von Stein gave the following answer:

"The journey was made for the sake of being dazzled. People take pomp for strength, fearful weakness for prudence, and are glad of a few moments' rest to hide their eyes from the future, which has nothing to promise but a miserable and humiliating existence."

It may be that the reception at St. Petersburg was not without designed intention on the part of the Russian court, and it may have had a lulling influence on the royal pair; but certainly the amiable attentions which were showered upon them were sincere, and it is clear that the heart of the queen was not in all this pomp,

Louisa wrote immediately after the anniversary of her birthday, March 12, 1809:

" My birthday was a fearful day to me. A splendid banquet was given by the city in my honor in the evening; before that there had been an abundant and handsome repast in the palace. Oh, how sad it made me! My heart was torn. I smiled, and said pleasant things to those who gave the banquet. I made myself agreeable to every body, yet I did not know where to turn for grief. To whom will Prussia belong at the end of the year? Where shall we all be scattered? Almighty Father, have mercy upon us!"

The king and queen were prevented from returning to Berlin at this time on account of the new war with Austria. They therefore returned to Königsberg, and took possession of a small estate called Hufen, situated in a secluded but delightful valley. Louisa's health was in a bad condition at this time, and the misfortune of Austria, which completed the servitude of Germany, prostrated her still more. She said, almost in despair, "God only knows where I shall die. I fear I will not be on Prussian soil."

The occasion of the baptism of the youngest child in October, 1809, was a painful day to her on account of the minister's dull, soulless, rationalistic discourse. He had no idea of the power of the sacrament, knew nothing of the covenant made with God, through baptism, into the death of Christ; his only idea was that of a consecration of the child on its entrance into life. The queen could not be comforted until it was proved to her, from the works of the writers of the Protestant Church, that the power of baptism did not depend altogether upon those who administered it. She saw in the prevailing skepticism fresh cause for the misfortune of Prussia. "We have sunk because we have let go," she said. This warned her anew not to become weary of laboring for the religious elevation of the people. The renowned minister Von Stein entered quite into the views of the king and queen, and stated that the most important task now was "to encourage a moral, religious, patriotic spirit in the nation."

The queen, after her return from St. Petersburg, was full of longings to be again in Berlin. In August she wrote :

" Since my health will allow it, we go on the 12th to Pillau. O that it were to Berlin ! A home-sickness that I cannot describe draws me thither, and to my Charlottenburg !"

On the 15th of December a return to Berlin was really decided upon, and yet she looked forward to it with a certain feeling of sadness. She could not tell why she had this feeling in reference to a journey she so much desired.

" So I shall soon be in Berlin again," she wrote, "and return to so many true hearts that love and esteem me. My joy in the thought is so great that I shed tears whenever I think of finding every thing as it was. And yet every thing will be so different, that I cannot now conceive what I shall do. Dark anticipations trouble me ; but I hope things will be pleasanter than I anticipate."

The joyous reception which the royal couple met every-where on their way to Berlin, manifested how little the late troubles had destroyed the love which had existed between the people and the ruling dynasty. Their entry into Berlin occurred the same day on which, sixteen years before, Louisa had entered a happy bride. The tears of the queen fell like burning drops into the hearts of the best of the people.

The great and good Ernst Moritz Arndt wrote :

"More eyes were wet with tears of sorrow than joy. The deep grief of the beautiful queen was evident in the midst of her joy as she stood at the window acknowledging the people's greeting, for her eyes were red with weeping."

There is scarcely any other German who has

been so much applauded by his country as the author of the above paragraph. He was beloved for his Christian patriotism, which he strove to exhibit on every possible occasion. He sought in every way to arouse in the hearts of his fellow-countrymen a Christian and national spirit.

We find among his numerous writings a small work, which was written at this time, and entitled, "Catechism for the German Warrior," and from which we make a few extracts. He first gives a sketch of the history of Germany, and after describing the outrages of the French, he continues :

"It is now the will of God that this pride shall be curbed ; that the French shall be punished for the outrages that they have committed in every land, and which cry to Heaven. It is the will of God that the Germans shall arise in righteous indignation, and smite the tyrant, and regain the freedom which they inherited from their fathers. Yes, people of

Germany, God will give you love and trust, and you will see what you are, and what you ought to be. God will kindle a flame within your hearts and awaken the bold spirit of liberty that the enemy would fain cause to slumber. God himself will go before you, and be with your hosts, and bless your banners with victory, if you will only have faith in eternal justice, and believe that there is a God who will crush the tyrant. . . . Brave and pious heroes, it is in the power of Him to lift man out of and above himself, so that he scarcely knows what he has been or what he is. The arm of man is weak unless God lends it strength, and his heart is easily discouraged unless inspired with unconquerable faith."

The same spirit pervades every thing that he wrote at this time, and he endeavored with all his strength to keep Christ continually before the people as their light and their salvation. It was truly in connection with Christianity that this good man looked for the regeneration of his country, and which he was finally enabled to witness.*

"Father Arndt," as he was later called, died on the 29th of January, 1860, in his ninety-first year. He was followed to the grave by a vast procession of people, and the spot where he was interred had been selected by himself under an oak planted by his own hands. One of his own most beautiful hymns was sung, as he was committed to the earth, by loving friends. We give it as translated by Miss Winkworth, in the "Lyra Germanica:"

GO AND DIG MY GRAVE TO-DAY.

Go and dig my grave to-day:
   Weary of my wanderings all,
Now from earth I pass away,
   For the heavenly peace doth call;
Angel voices from above
Call me to their rest and love.

Go and dig my grave to-day:
   Homeward doth my journey tend,
And I lay my staff away
   Here where all things earthly end,

---

* Baur, *Religious Life in Germany*, vol. ii, pp. 252–57.

And I lay my weary head
On the only painless bed.

What yet is there I should do,
  Lingering in this darksome vale?
Proud and mighty, fair to view,
  Are our schemes, and yet they fail,
Like the sand before the wind,
That no power of man can bind.

Farewell, O ye much-loved friends,
  Grief hath smote you as a sword,
But the Comforter descends
  Unto them who love the Lord.
Weep not o'er a passing show,
To the' eternal world I go.

Weep not that I take my leave
  Of the world; that I exchange
Errors that too closely cleave,
  Shadows, empty ghosts that range
Through this world of naught and night
For a land of truth and light.

Weep not, my Redeemer lives;
  Heavenward, springing from the dust,
Clear-eyed Hope her comfort gives;
  Faith, Heaven's champion, bids me trust;
Love eternal whispers nigh,
Child of God, fear not to die.

In returning to Louisa, we find that the happiness that she had so much anticipated in returning to Berlin was not destined to be of long duration. Napoleon threatened to return with an army of extermination if the war contribution was not paid. Deep anguish gnawed at the very life of the queen. On the 10th of March, 1810, she said, sadly, "I think this will be the last birthday I shall ever celebrate." Presentiments of death were constantly in her mind. Only a short time did her failing health improve, and that was during her residence in Potsdam. She received the holy communion in Berlin at Easter with great faith. On the 20th of May she visited, for the last time, Paretz, where she had spent so many happy days, and from which she had been absent during so many weary years. She leaned upon the king's arm, and walked once more through the beautiful gardens and groves.

"That gate has never been opened since her death, and the date of this last visit,

13

surmounted by her initial letters, is wrought in its iron tracery. The walk has been carefully turfed, and bordered with flowers; and in the grotto on the banks of the Havel, where she used to sit and teach her children, is an iron table, on which is inscribed in letters of gold: 'Remember the absent.'"*

For several years it had been Louisa's wish to visit her father, the Duke of Strelitz; only once since her marriage had she been so situated as to be able to sleep under the paternal roof. On the 25th of June she started from Charlottenburg to carry this long-cherished wish into execution. She passed through Oranienburg to Fürstenburg, the first place within the boundaries of the dukedom of Strelitz. There her father, her youngest sister, and her two brothers were ready to receive her. On the journey thither Louisa was full of joy; but now her cheerfulness gave way to a strange seriousness, and then to sorrow, as though her

---

* " The Perfect Light," p. 122.

soul was moved with a dark foreboding that the tie which bound her to earth was very soon to be broken. The presence of the ducal family, who were standing ready to receive her, was a great surprise. She cried out in tears, " Oh, there is my father ! " and rushed into his arms.

At the entrance of the paternal castle, in Strelitz, the Landgravine of Hesse, who was now eighty-one years of age, waited to receive her granddaughter. Louisa sprang out of the carriage and embraced her venerable grandmother, the true patroness of her childhood. They both wept tears of joy, as well as of sorrow.

Louisa wished this visit to be given entirely to her relatives, and, therefore, set aside only one day for a public reception. As she appeared in the hall among the assembled people an indescribable loftiness of soul and mildness of manner seemed to pervade her being. Her beautiful, noble features bore the impress of great·sorrow, and when she involuntarily cast her eyes upward, they seemed to bespeak a longing for her heavenly home.   Once an impressive silence reigned; those present dared not speak of the sorrowful past, in which the chastening hand of God had been manifested. A lady broke the painful silence by approaching the queen, and expressing her admiration at an exquisite necklace of pearls that Louisa wore—her only ornament.

"Yes," answered the queen, "I love them very much.   These are all I have reserved, after having given all my other jewelry for the good of the kingdom.   They are so appropriate, for they signify *tears*, of which I have shed so many."

The king's arrival on the 28th of June completed the joy of the queen.

"Now I am," she said, "quite happy for the first time since I came here!"

It was indeed a moment of general joy, saddened only by Louisa's illness.   After the first excitement of the re-union had subsided, she sat down to her father's writing-table and wrote :

"MY DEAR FATHER, — I am to-day very happy as your daughter, and as the wife of the best of men.   LOUISA.

"NEW STRELITZ, 28*th of June*, 1810."

These were the last words that she ever wrote, and they are preserved by her son, the present German emperor, as a sacred relic.

XV.

Illness and Death.

THAT Louisa might enjoy more quietly the society of her family after the arrival of the king, they removed to the duke's castle of Hohenzieritz. She began immediately to suffer from fever and pain in her head. As she was not accustomed to notice trifling ailments, she made her appearance at the tea-table, and walked with the family in the garden in the evening. The following morning the physician found her in a very critical condition. On being bled she rallied, so that the king felt it safe to leave her. Pressing State business demanded his presence in Berlin, and he left, promising to return in a few days. During the course of the week her sickness seemed to decrease. She bore with patience the sleepless nights, and her mind remained calm.

The king was taken ill at Charlottenburg, and could not return as soon as he expected. He sent, however, the celebrated physician and surgeon, Dr. Heim, to his beloved wife, and he pronounced the greatest danger past. But on the following day she was again worse. A letter that she received from the king affected her very much. She laid it next her heart, and exclaimed, "Oh what a letter! How happy the one who receives such a letter!"

She talked much of her precious children, and all proofs of sympathy in her sickness were fully appreciated, and afforded her great pleasure. Letters came daily from Berlin, expressive of the most heartfelt concern for her welfare. Louisa's sister, the Princess of Solms, watched constantly at her bedside, and would not leave her. This devotion on the part of the princess caused Louisa much anxiety, and she insisted that her sister should take certain hours for rest. She was also concerned about the health of her father and her grandmother, and often sighed, "Oh, if only their anxiety for me were not so great! It will make them ill!"

Toward the close of the week her condition seemed to be improved, and on Saturday, and Sunday especially, she appeared so free from pain that she was herself so joyfully certain of her convalescence that all entertained the most sanguine hopes of her recovery.

But on Monday morning she was suddenly attacked with severe spasms, which, in spite of all aid, lasted five hours. The physician saw that it was an incurable affection of the heart, and, therefore, prepared the father for the death of his daughter. The duke sent couriers in great haste for the king. Louisa repeatedly asked, "Will he soon come? How late is it?" She was very patient under her great pain, and whenever she felt the least relief, she thanked her heavenly Father with childlike confidence. The frailty of all earthly greatness, which she had experienced during her life, seemed to impress itself upon her more forcibly than ever. Once she said, "I am queen, and yet cannot move my arm."

During one of these painful hours she said to her physician, "Think of my dying, and leaving the king and my children!"

The cramps and pressure on her breast increased on the night of Wednesday, the 18th of July. Toward three o'clock her father was called, as he had commanded, and when he saw how much worse she had become, he said devoutly, "Lord, thy ways are not our ways."

About an hour later the king arrived with his two eldest sons. It was a dull morning, the sky being overcast. When Louisa heard of their arrival she was full of joy at the thought of seeing her loved ones once more. The king learned from the physician the certainty of her approaching dissolution, and was overwhelmed with grief. When the grandmother said that "nothing was impossible with

God," he uttered bitter words of sorrow, for he seemed to think he was doomed to misfortune:

" Oh if she were not mine she would live ; but since she is my wife she will surely die !"

He hastened from the chamber of death in order to compose himself. The queen then said,

" Tell him not to be so much agitated, or I shall die instantly."

He composed himself, and remained alone with her until another cramp seized her, when, although the physician came in immediately, he was unable to afford her relief. The king sat on the bed and held her right hand, while her sister held her left. The head of the sufferer lay on the breast of her dear friend, the Frau Von Berg. She said feebly,

" Nothing can relieve me now but death."

At ten minutes before nine, on the morning of the 19th of July, 1810, when her head sank back, and her eyes closed, she whispered, " Lord Jesus, make it short." Her prayer was

answered. Five minutes later, and her purified spirit left its earthly tenement and fled to
its heavenly home.

The king had sank down, overcome with
grief, but he soon raised himself again and
closed the sightless eyes of his beloved Louisa.
He then hastened and brought his two sons,
the crown prince and Prince William. They
fell on their knees by the bedside and bedewed
the hands of their mother with their burning
tears. The king and the duke fell into each
other's arms, and remained long embraced.
Louisa's features remained beautiful even in
death. A halo seemed now to hover about
her brow, and on her lips were victory and
peace. This is still to be seen in the portrait
taken immediately after her death, which is
preserved in the castle of Monbijou in Berlin.

" On examination it was found that a poly-
pus, with spreading branches, had grown into
her heart, out of which it had crushed the life.
Thus, literally, she had died of a broken heart.

"The news of the queen's death, at the early age of thirty-four, caused the deepest sorrow throughout the land. And as the death-knell was sounded in city and hamlet, the praise of her saintly virtues was on every lip, and grief for her untimely fate, caused, as it was universally believed, by the miseries of the war, was the burden of every heart." *

The announcement of her death was made in feeling terms from all the pulpits in the kingdom. We give here the earnest expressions of one of the clergy, which indicates the spirit of all :—

"Great have been the blessings that this country has enjoyed through the goodness of our remarkable queen. How can our hearts cease to thrill with love and gratitude as we recall the fidelity which she has shown to our country, and the pure example that she has left behind ? She has fought her last earthly battle, and now wears a far brighter crown than

* "The Perfect Light," pp. 128–9.

that earthly one that she wore with so much
dignity and grace while here below. May
trust in God alleviate the unutterable grief of
our king! May he go forward in his clearly
defined path, trusting in the same Providence
that has blessed him in the past! May the
pure spirit of the departed queen be poured
out in rich measure on the crown prince, who
is to be our ruler in future years! His tears
fall thickly over his deceased mother, and well
they may, for he has lost in her the greatest
human support of his life. May he have the
same trust in God which his sainted mother
enjoyed! May our beloved Fatherland receive
from Heaven all those rich blessings which the
patriotic Louisa invoked upon it! and may all
our countrymen aspire to the greatness and
goodness of her life!"

On the 27th of July her royal remains were
conveyed to Berlin and placed in the cathedral.
From there, on the 23d of December, they
were removed to their last resting-place at ·

Charlottenburg, and were followed by a long concourse of people. A contemporary wrote :

"Each family seemed and felt as sad as though it had lost one of its own members. Countless tears were shed as the hearse passed on which bore her precious remains. The greater portion of the inhabitants were clad in mourning. Through all Prussia, nay, through all Germany, was felt the deepest grief, so dear was this beloved queen to the people. She had given a noble example to the whole German Fatherland of piety, purity, simplicity, domestic virtue, humility in prosperity, courage in times of misfortune; in short, an example of a true and unblemished life, in small as well as great things, until death."

"The king sought in every way to give expression to the true and tender love which had given the charm to his life. He always wore the portrait of the queen concealed in the decoration of the Black Eagle. Her beautiful bust, which was modeled by Rauch, was placed above

his bed, on which he spread with his own
hands, before retiring to rest, a shawl that she
had been accustomed to wear.   Her toilette
service was arranged in the adjoining room as
she left it, with her Bible beside it—the book
in which she had found such comfort and joy."

The king desired to connect the memory of
his deceased Louisa with works of Christian
love, on which her name could be bestowed.
He consulted with Bishop Eylert, and ulti-
mately two institutions were founded, the *Lou-
isen-denkmal*, and the *Louisen-stiftung*.   The
denkmal, or memorial, was designed to com-
memorate the matrimonial happiness which the
king and queen had enjoyed.   A fund was set
apart which furnished three hundred dollars a
year, to be divided between three bridal couples.   The royal bounty was given every year
on the . 19th of July, at nine o'clock in the
morning, the day and hour of Queen Louisa's death.   The king was very particular
that the greatest care should be taken in the

selection of those persons who were the most deserving.

The *Louisen-stiftung*, or Louisa's institution, was a work of far wider scope. It was, in reality, founded on Louisa's own desire, expressed to the king on their return from St. Petersburg, where she had seen the institution founded by the Empress Dowager of Russia, for the benefit of ladies in reduced circumstances; those among them who were still young were educated as governesses.

The iron cross, with its motto, "With God for King and Country," worn with such pride by citizens of all classes who distinguished themselves in the war of liberation, was instituted by the king in 1814, on Louisa's birthday; and the *Louisen-orden*, or Order of Louisa, was established in the same year, on the anniversary of his birth. The following words, taken from his address on the occasion, sufficiently describe his purpose in founding this order:

" Our women, inspired with the noblest courage, have cheerfully yielded their husbands and sons for the defense of the fatherland. By their soothing care the sufferings of the sick and wounded have been alleviated, their sympathy has given consolation and support. Therefore we have determined to do honor to the female sex, and to testify our high esteem for noble women, by creating an order to be worn by them."

The insignia of the order is a golden cross, with the letter L in black enamel on an azure ground, the letter being encircled by stars. On the back of the cross are engraved the dates 1813 and 1814. Like the Iron Cross, it is worn with a white ribbon, and fastened with a bow on the left breast. Young and old women are alike eligible for this distinction, the number being limited to one hundred.

The order, like that of the Iron Cross, is open to all classes. The obligation lies on the committee to collect the fullest possible ac-

14

count of the most devoted services done by women throughout the kingdom of Prussia, and, after thorough examination, to choose the worthiest, and present them to the king.*

The king made the Princess William of Prussia, who was an intimate friend of the queen, the directress of this order. The fitness of the selection lay in the remarkable resemblance between the princess and the queen, and in the love and affection that the former entertained for the latter. The following passage from a letter, written immediately after Louisa's death by the Princess William to the Baron Von Stein, is an affecting witness to the real reverence and love in which the princess held the queen :—

"BERLIN, *Dec.* 14, 1810.

"It is impossible to explain every thing in writing ; but I should so much like to tell you how all the attractiveness of life is over for me, now that our beloved queen is gone.

* Hudson, *Lousia, Queen of Prussia.* Vol. II, p. 343.

She was so unspeakably kind and sisterly to
me that I miss her every moment, and with
every fresh event. How I regret every word
that I may ever have spoken against her, since
I have clearly seen that it could only have
been envy which induced me to do it, because
she was so much better than I.

"The king is worthy of all reverence in this
sorrow, which will last with his life; he shows
so much Christian resignation and patience;
he is so kind to me that I can scarcely look at
him without tears."

We can say of Louisa what King Max of
Bavaria said with truth of this same Princess
William, his mother-in-law:

> "Star and crown of German women,
>   Go in peace unto thy rest;
> Near the throne, yet only seeking
>   How to serve thy Lord the best.
> *   *   *   *   *
> "In those bitter days of pain,
>   When the scourge our country beat,
> Binding Europe with his chain,
>   Bringing princes to his feet;

Keenly, truly, did she feel,
    Trembling for her country's fame,
And with love and faithful zeal
    Strove for freedom's holy name.

" Stood with angel love untiring
    Where the wounded warrior lay,
While her youthful smiles inspiring,
    Cheered the victor on his way.

*   *   *   *   *

" Now on you, ye German women,—
    What she was ye surely know,—
Still is Germany depending
    In the hour of trial and woe ;
Cherish zeal's inspiring flame,
    For your country's fame and good;
We are one in birth and name ;
    Tie the bonds of brotherhood."

XVI.

The Country and the King.

STEFFENS relates the impression which the death of the queen made at Halle, which then belonged to the kingdom of Westphalia:

" There was a commotion in the town during the first days after the news, which was only equaled by that caused by the overthrow of the Prussian armies in the late war. Grief was depicted upon every countenance ; there was mourning in every house, and every body seemed impressed with a feeling that the nation's last faint hope had departed with the life of this adored woman. Her death was generally ascribed to the unhappy condition of the country. Many said to themselves, the enemy has slain the guardian angel of the

people ; and a feeling of revenge, and an un-
spoken oath to keep her memory in inviolable
constancy, strengthened the national resolve to
seize every opportunity to throw off the odious
yoke."

The queen remained after her death, as before, the heroine of a war which the people
were determined to bring to a successful issue.

The influence of this good woman did not
die with her.   Her spirit seemed to be at work
in the last defeat ; and what Körner sang in
the year 1813,

" Luise schwebe segnend um den Gatten," *

was the expression of the general feeling of all
who loved her—that from the rest which was
granted to her the departed one could behold
with glorified eyes the conflicts in which her
husband   and   the   nation   were   engaged.
Fouqué, Schenkendorf, and others, as well as
Körner, have tuned their harps in her praise.

* Louisa, o'er thy consort blessings shed.

The king, who had sunk into the deepest grief on account of his defeats, received now the heaviest blow by the death of the queen. To the Count Henkel von Donnersmark, on their first meeting, he could only say the following words : " This is the hardest blow."

Bowed down by this affliction he passed the next year of his life, and then, trusting in God, he began the new war against Napoleon like a knight avenging his insulted beloved one. Arndt says :

" The king had the gifts of uprightness, bravery, and piety, but he was chilling and reserved. In his quiet, plain appearance and gesture there was an expression of deep sadness ; he was the sorrowful knight, who could not forget his lost loved one. Never could he forget his beloved Louisa, who was snatched away in the bloom of her loveliness, killed by the trouble and misfortunes of the times. Since that time, in 1810, when she died in her Mecklenburg home, his face has never beamed with pleasure. He was scarcely able to enjoy with his subjects the rejoicing consequent on the victories of 1813, 1814, and 1815, but lived in the solitude of his own heart and its sorrow. As Beatrice, lost to Dante for this life, was his guide to heaven, and became to him the glorified personification of a saving knowledge of God, so the image of the glorified queen hovered before the eyes of the king, not only as that of his beloved spouse, but as an impersonation of all the grief suffered on account of their country, and the struggles to be surmounted in its behalf. It really was the case, that the king fought against Napoleon not only for his kingdom, but for the honor of his beloved one."

When the king went to the war he took with him some small articles that had belonged to his beloved Louisa. Every thing that she possessed when living was doubly dear to him now. From the victorious field of Leipzig he hastened to Berlin; his steps were first turned toward the cathedral, where, with the people, he gave thanks to God. As soon as he could escape from the crowd he hastened to Charlottenburg, to the grave of the queen, uncovered his head, laid the laurel wreath which he had brought with him upon the tomb, and remained in silent prayer. He then returned to the army.

It is probable that the tumultuous events which the king had passed through from 1806 to 1814 had deepened and strengthened his faith.

He still adhered to those strict religious views which he expressed to minister Von Wöllner on assuming the reins of government :—

"I honor religion myself, and willingly follow its blessed precepts, and should be very sorry to rule over a nation which had no religion ; but I know that it is, and always must be, a matter of the heart, and of the feelings, and of personal conviction, and that it is to forward the cause of virtue and righteousness among men.

It must not be degraded into a meaningless babble by any formal compulsion. Reason and philosophy must be its inseparable companions. It will then be able to stand secure of itself, without needing the authority of those who claim the right to impose their doctrines on future generations, and to dictate to posterity what it is to think in every age, and under all circumstances, upon subjects which have the most powerful influence upon its well being."

When at Königsberg, after the great defeat, he had a desire for the word of God. Barowsky, afterward archbishop, was there with this most powerful source of comfort. He read and explained to the king the striking narratives of the book of Daniel, and the seeds of a firm faith were sown in his agitated mind. He remained true to his opinion, that religion must be a matter "of the heart, and of the feelings, and of personal conviction."

"The most barren and miserable view which

a man can possibly hold of Christianity and its divine ordinances," said the king, "is that wise and enlightened people will hold religion in reverence, because, although quite superfluous to the educated, it is necessary and good for keeping the middle and lower classes in order by means of the superstition which it instills; the higher and highest classes require no such bugbear. If this is enlightenment, I do not know what obscurity is. It is like a sunstroke, which takes away your senses."

"His piety," says Baur, "was an affair of the heart and of personal conviction. He could not dispense with it in his conflict with sin, for the patient bearing of the cross, and the hope of everlasting life. He loved the Bible with the love which is peculiar to the Protestant Christian. He did not explain away its doctrines. He had a deep feeling of the sinfulness of the human race, and therefore full confidence in the mercy of Jesus Christ. He was earnest in prayer, for he knew that prayer is heard, and

13

can accomplish much when it is earnest. He
could not dispense with public worship. He
felt it beneficial to join with his people on
the same level. He rejected flattery with real
indignation, especially if it ventured to address him in holy places. The house of the
Lord was holy to him, because he knew that
there divine love condescends to meet the
humble confessor of sin and the faithful pe-
titioner for divine mercy in the proclamation
of the word and the administration of the
sacrament.

"The simplicity of his character developed
itself in sacred things, in the humility of the
sinner, who, like all other men, can only live
by faith. But though his faith was firm in the
atonement of Jesus Christ, his Christianity had
a thoroughly moral tendency, as a genuine
Gospel faith always has. The king was up-
right in the highest degree. He was diligent
in his calling, after the hereditary principle of
Prussian monarchs, that a king should consider

himself the chief servant of the State ; benevolent, with royal generosity ; having a tender
sympathy for special cases of distress ; chaste
in word and deed, and especially severe upon
transgressors of the seventh commandment ;
and animated by a powerful impulse to labor
for the general good. He strove to attain to
that attribute of charity that 'seeketh not her
own.' But above all other things, it was his
desire to revive among his people an apprecia-
tion of religion, which had, unfortunately, so
much declined, by openly acknowledging his
adherence to divine truth. This effort was the
origin of the Holy Alliance, which Frederic
William entered into after the victory with the
Emperors of Russia and Austria, and of which
he was perhaps the originator.

"'My comfort in disquiet, my hope in God,'
was the superscription of his will, an appropriate motto for a king who had seen so much
adversity both in peace and war, but who had
struggled against it with a conscientious mind,

and whose consolation was the prospect of that rest which remaineth for the people of God." *

Louisa was buried within a small Doric temple at the extremity of a shady walk, in a retired part of the garden at Charlottenburg.

In this same place there had stood a temple or summer-house, as we should call it, built in the Grecian style of architecture. The queen had habitually frequented this secluded spot, to enjoy quiet recreation and refreshment with her husband and children. To the king that temple and its site now seemed sacred to the memory of the departed one. He had the little edifice removed to Peacock's Island, and on the spot where it had stood he raised another, somewhat similar in style, but far superior in construction, and built of rare and durable materials. A flight of eight steps leads up through the iron door to the interior of the mausoleum ; the exterior is of red granite, and four highly polished Doric pillars support the

* "Religious Life in Germany," pp. 104, 5.

entablature. The Alpha and Omega (A—Ω) on the façade of the triangular pediment are suggestive of Him who holds 'the spirits of the departed in safe keeping :

" *I am he that liveth, and was dead ; and, behold, I am alive for evermore. Amen.*"

In this last abode the remains of Queen Louisa were deposited. It was exactly one year since she had returned to Berlin after the calamities of war, and seventeen years since she entered the Prussian capital as a bride. Sunbeams and shadows cast their checkered shade on this sepulchral edifice. The dark grove or wood of larch trees which forms the inclosing avenue, though thickly planted, cannot exclude the light of day, or even the moonshine of night. This little temple is sheltered on all sides by trees—pines and larches, yews and cypresses—and among them some which annually shed their leaves, to tell of peace in decay, of hope in death, of joy in resurrection.

Within this exquisitely beautiful mausoleum

rests the figure of the beloved queen, with the hands folded naturally upon the breast, and in an attitude of profound repose. "She seems not dead, but sleeping; and the great artist, Bottiger, said he dared not speak lest he should awaken the blessed spirit to a world of care.

"The Prussian eagle at the foot of the sarcophagus, showing that she belonged to the house of Hohenzollern, was modeled from a magnificent bird taken captive in the Apennines.

"This monument is the masterpiece of the sculptor Rauch, who worked it out under the inspiration of love and grief, for he shared the general feeling of enthusiasm for this sainted woman, who had fostered his rising genius." *

When the king was meditating upon erecting a superb monument to the memory of his departed Louisa, he thought of employing Canova; but Rauch, who had earnestly desired

* "The Perfect Light," p. 82.

and hoped to do it, took the disappointment so much to heart, that, with Canova's consent, the work was transferred to him. Rauch returned from Berlin to Italy to execute the design, dividing his time between Carrara and Rome.

An extraordinary adventure befell this beautiful piece of sculpture. The ship that was conveying it from Italy was captured by an American privateer, and re-taken by an English vessel, whose commander put the monument safely on shore at Jersey, whence it was forwarded to Hamburg. Rauch, when traveling homeward by land, read, at Munich, an account of the capture of his work. Despairing of its recovery, he was on the point of returning to Italy to recommence his labor, when he heard that the sculpture had reached its destination.

On the fifth anniversary of Queen Louisa's death the mausoleum was opened to receive this beautiful work of art. The admiration that it attracted soon gave Rauch a European reputation. Germany acknowledges him as the greatest sculptor she has ever produced, and his numerous works are scattered over that country, divided among the chief cities of the empire, Berlin, however, having the greater part.

King Frederic William III. survived his beloved Louisa thirty years. He died on the 7th of June, 1840, having reigned forty-three years. A long and glorious reign it was, though heavily clouded through the years from Jena to Waterloo. It was also an eventful and prosperous reign, for, notwithstanding the misfortunes against which he had to contend, he was permitted to have the satisfaction of leaving the country more extensive, more powerful, and more wealthy than it had ever been before.

The aged monarch, who had attained his seventieth year, was very dear to his people, and they could not endure the thought of parting with him. His spirit passed gently away, and his remains were conveyed to Charlottenburg, and laid beside those of Queen Louisa. His statue, "with his martial cloak around him," was placed over the sarcophagus by his son, the crown prince. It was executed by Rauch. On either side is a marble candelabrum, that with the Fates by Rauch, and that with the Three Muses by Tieck.

In the whole mausoleum, indeed, we see a monument bearing witness to the artistic genius, the pure taste, and the high religious feeling of his son, Frederic William IV., who improved on and completed what his father had begun. He made it beautiful as it is, and hallowed it with many a text of Scripture. Turn which way you will the eye is attracted by some glorious promise, or some striking words which assure us of the indissoluble connection between this transitory life and life eternal.*

* Cf. Hudson, *Louisa, Queen of Prussia*, vol. ii, pp. 366–

Can we wonder that the mausoleum of Charlottenburg is one of the most attractive places to the Prussian people?

THE QUEEN OF PRUSSIA'S TOMB.

BY FELICIA HEMANS.

IT stands where northern willows weep,
    A temple fair and lone;
Soft shadows o'er its marble sweep,
    From cypress branches thrown;
While silently around it spread,
Thou feel'st the presence of the dead.

And what within is richly shrined?
    A sculptured woman's form,
Lovely, in perfect rest reclined,
    As one beyond the storm:
Yet not of death, but slumber, lies
The solemn sweetness of those eyes.

The folded hands, the calm, pure face,
    The mantle's quiet flow,
The gentle yet majestic grace
    Throned on the matron brow;
These, in that scene of tender gloom,
With a still glory, robe the tomb.

There stands an eagle, at the feet
　Of the fair image wrought ;
A kingly emblem—not unmeet
　To wake yet deeper thought ;
She whose high heart finds rest below
Was royal in her birth and woe.

There are pale garlands hung above,
　Of dying scent and hue ;
She was a mother—in her love
　How sorrowfully true !
Oh ! hallowed long be every leaf,
The record of her children's grief :

She saw their birthright's warrior-crown
　Of olden glory spoiled,
The standard of their sire's borne down,
　The shield's bright blazon soiled ;
She met the tempest meekly brave,
Then turned o'erwearied to the grave.

She slumbered, but it came—it came,
　Her land's redeeming hour,
With the glad shout and signal flame
　Sent on from tower to tower,
Fast through the realm a spirit moved,
'Twas hers, the lofty and the loved !

Then was her name a note that rung
　To rouse bold hearts from sleep ;
Her memory. as a banner flung
　Forth by the Baltic deep ;

Her grief, a bitter vial poured
To sanctify the avenger's sword.

And the crowned eagle spread again
    Her pinion to the sun ;
And the strong land shook off its chain,
    So was the triumph won !
But woe for earth, where sorrow's tone
Still blends with Victory's—*She* was gone.

Glaucia.
A Story of Athens in the First Century. By Emma
Leslie. Illustrated. 12mo $1 25

Talks with Girls.
By Augusta Larned. 12mo 1 50

Peter, the Apprentice.
An Historical Tale of the Reformation in England. By
the author of "Faithful, but not Famous," etc. 16mo.   90

Romance without Fiction.
Or, Sketches from the Portfolio of an Old Missionary.
By Rev. Henry Bleby. 12mo 1 75

The Man of One Book;
Or, the Life of the Rev. William Marsh, D.D. By his
Daughter. Edited by Daniel Wise. 12mo 1 50

Sunday Afternoons.
A Book for Little People. By E. F. Burr, D.D., author
of "Ecce-Celum." 16mo 75

Little Princess,
And other Stories, chiefly about Christmas. By Aunt
Hattie. 18mo 65

School-Life of Ben and Bentie.
Illustrated. 18mo 90

Peeps at our Sunday-Schools.
By Rev. Alfred Taylor. 12mo 1 25

Elizabeth Tudor:
The Queen and the Woman. By Virginia F. Town-
send. Illustrated. 12mo 1 50

True Stories of the American Fathers.
For the Girls and Boys all over the Land. By Miss
Rebecca M'Conkey. Illustrated. 12mo 1 50

Glimpses of our Lake Region in 1863,
And other Papers. By Mrs. H. C. Gardner. 12mo... 1 50

Through the Eye to the Heart;
Or, Eye-Teaching in the Sunday-School. By Rev. W.
F. Crafts. 12mo 1 50

Discontent,
And other Stories. By Mrs. H. C. Gardner. 12mo... 1 25

The Story of a Pocket Bible.
Ten illustrations. 12mo....... ....$1 25

Historical Souvenirs of Martin Luther.
By Charles W. Hubner. Illustrated. 12mo..... 1 00

Words that Shook the World ;
Or, Martin Luther his own Biographer. By Charles
Adams, D D. Twenty-two Illustrations. 12mo.. 1 25

Renata of Este.
From the German of Rev. Carl Strack. By Catherine E. Hurst. 16mo................ .... 1 25

Anecdotes of the Wesleys.
By J. B. Wakeley, D.D. 12mo 1 25

Martyrs to the Tract Cause.
A contribution to the History of the Reformation.
By J. F. Hurst, D.D. 12mo................... 75

Palissy, the Huguenot Potter.
By C. L. Brightwell. Illustrated. 16mo......... 1 25

Prince of Pulpit Orators.
A Portraiture of Rev. George Whitefield, M.A. By
J. B. Wakeley, D.D. 12mo................... 1 25

Thomas Chalmers.
A Biographical Study. By James Dodds. 12mo. 1 00

Gustavus Adolphus.
The Hero of the Reformation. From the French
of L. Abelous. By Mrs. C. A. Lacroix. Illustrated.
12mo.. 1 00

William the Taciturn.
From the French of L. Abelous. By Professor J.
P. Lacroix. Illustrated. 16mo................. 1 25

Life of Oliver Cromwell.
By Charles Adams, D.D. 16mo................. 1 25

Lady Huntington Portrayed.
By Rev Z. A. Mudge. 12mo................... 1 25

Curiosities of Animal Life.
Recent Discoveries of the Microscope. 12mo..... 0 75